POWER

Praise for The Book of Secrets

'Fast paced and thrilling.'

Irish Independent

'A brilliant fantasy fairy tale story set in modern-day Ireland.'

Sunday Independent

ALEX DUNNE is an Irish author living in Canada. She spends her time thinking up magical tales for children, teens and adults and drinking far too much tea. Alex has a BA in English & History from the University of Limerick and an MA in Literature & Publishing from NUI Galway. She is a co-founder of *Silver Apples* magazine, an online literary journal dedicated to showcasing the best of Irish and international writing. *The Book of Secrets*, Cat and Shane's first adventure, won the Eilís Dillon Award at the KPMG Children's Books Ireland Awards in 2023. You can follow Alex on Twitter and Instagram @alexdunnewrites

The Harp of Power

Alex Dunne

THE O'BRIEN PRESS
DUBLIN

First published in 2023 by
The O'Brien Press Ltd,
12 Terenure Road East, Rathgar,
Dublin 6, D06 HD27 Ireland.

Tel: +353 1 4923333; Fax: +353 1 4922777

E-mail: books@obrien.ie
Website: obrien.ie

The O'Brien Press is a member of Publishing Ireland
ISBN: 978-1-78849-448-9

1 3 5 7 8 6 4 2
24 25 26 23

Cover illustration by Shona Shirley Macdonald
Design and internal illustrations by Emma Byrne

Printed and bound by Norhaven A/S, Denmark.

Published in

DUBLIN

UNESCO
City of Literature

For Richard who cheers me on every step of the way.

Contents

From the Darkness of the Well

It was dark at the bottom of the well, so dark that Cethlenn never knew whether it was night or day, and that was just how she liked it.

Her world consisted of little more than damp stone walls coated with centuries of mould and slime and the snuffling sounds of mice and voles who would occasionally pass through her lair. No creature ever stayed long in the well and that was also to her liking. After thousands of years, Cethlenn simply wanted to be left alone with her memories.

It had not always been this way. Once upon a time,

Cethlenn was a warrior and a queen. Her people were a mighty tribe known as the Fomorians, and they worshipped her for her cruelty and her cunning. For many years, she led the Fomorians into combat with spear in hand and her beloved husband Balor by her side. The mere sight of them on the battlefield was enough make grown men and women tremble and weep. Together, Cethlenn and Balor ruled the land with an iron fist, until one day, a new tribe landed on the rocky shores of their island kingdom.

They called themselves the Tuatha Dé Danann – the people of the Goddess Danu – and they set about conquering the Fomorians' land. Cethlenn and Balor did not take such an insult to their rule lightly, and soon the two tribes began to clash. The Tuatha Dé Danann were strong, but so were the Fomorians, and neither tribe was able to gain the upper hand. So it remained until the fateful day the two forces met on the fields of Moytura for their final battle.

It was a memory that would live on in Cethlenn's mind forever because it was the day she lost everything – her husband, her kingdom and her purpose. The Tuatha Dé

Danann had finally defeated the Fomorians and become the rulers of the land of Ireland.

Cethlenn survived the Battle of Moytura and went into hiding, trying to process her grief. Through her long years of isolation, she often thought back to that day and wondered how different it might have been if only her plans had come to fruition, if the Fomorians had been able to hold onto the treasure they had stolen from the Tuatha Dé Danann…

In time, her sadness turned to anger, which burned white-hot inside her. Soon, her only thought was of revenge.

For many years, she roamed the land from shore to shore, over mountains and through valleys, waiting for her chance to strike, but her enemies were powerful, and she was alone, a shadow of her former self. As time wore on, her flesh decayed and her bones became dust and Cethlenn found herself as little more than a spirit, trapped somewhere between life and death, but still her anger fuelled her, even if there was nothing she could do but watch and wait.

She would slip into the Tuatha Dé Danann's strongholds, an unseen shadow, and do her best learn all she could about her enemies and how they might be defeated. She became convinced that the way to defeat them lay with the very treasure that the Fomorians had tried to steal away all those years ago. But Cethlenn was just a spirit and without a body, what could she do?

Eventually, all things must end, even the reign of the mighty Tuatha Dé Danann. The day came when they were forced to retreat to the Otherworld, far away from Cethlenn and her schemes. For the first time in centuries, Cethlenn was truly alone, a ghost among an unfamiliar people, with all hope of vengeance gone.

It was then that she found the well. Cethlenn knew that wells are in-between places, trapped somewhere between the Otherworld and the mortal realm, just as she herself was, and it seemed as good a place as any to wait out the rest of eternity.

For a time, her peace would occasionally be disturbed by pilgrims who believed the well to be a holy place and came in search of blessings from the water. But they had not come by for many years. Like Cethlenn, the well was largely forgotten. And so she was alone in her silence.

Until one day, she heard a voice.

'It has to be around here somewhere. Are you sure you don't smell anything?'

The sound came as a shock to Cethlenn. She could not remember the last time she had heard a voice – a *human* voice – and so close to her!

'Nothing yet. Sorry, Becca. If it was here, I'd know. Nothing gets past *these* nostrils!' said a second voice – an animal voice, Cethlenn noted, and yet it seemed to be speaking directly to the human... She should ignore them. What did she care for humans and their ways? But after so many years with nothing but her own regrets to keep her company, Cethlenn couldn't help but be intrigued. She allowed herself to drift up the well, just a bit, so she could better hear their conversation.

'I don't get it,' said the human – Becca, she supposed. 'According to the map, the holy well should be right here.'

'Pfft, map shmap!' said the animal. 'Come on, it's getting late and I'm starving! Let's just go and... oh! Wait a second, what do we have here?'

'Have you found it?' the human's voice raised to an excited pitch.

'Hang on, let me just... eeewww! Yuck, that is definitely the smell of stinky old well water. It's right over here, Becca.'

The human squealed and suddenly, Cethlenn's world was ripped apart. A beam of sunlight lit up the well for a moment before it was covered up again by the face of a young woman peering down at her. Cethlenn almost shrank back before remembering that this woman couldn't see her. Shame flooded through her. How far she had fallen from her days as a warrior queen.

'Well done, Vinnie! You're getting an extra mouse for dinner tonight.'

Becca's face disappeared from the hole and a smaller, furrier face appeared in her place. It looked to Cethlenn like a pine marten, or perhaps a stoat.

'Woohoo!' said the small creature Cethlenn now knew to be called Vinnie. 'Want me to start digging this up? As well as being an expert sniffer I am, in fact, a world-class digger.'

'I know you are,' said Becca. Cethlenn could almost *hear* the smile in her voice, and it made her sick. 'But let's leave it as it is for now. It's already getting dark, and

I don't want to risk disturbing the magic. We have the location so we can always come back another day and open it up properly...'

Becca was saying something else, but Cethlenn was no longer paying attention. She had spoken of magic. *Magic.* Hearing the word uttered on mortal lips set her mind aflame. Could this human woman know something of the old ways? How could that be? Back in Cethlenn's time humans were pathetic creatures, made to be ruled. She moved closer now, her spirit pressed against the opening of the well, desperate to learn more.

'So this is definitely the right well?' asked Vinnie.

'I can't be sure until I get some of the water and run some tests,' said Becca, 'but I think so. There's something about this place... I can almost feel the air humming with old magic. Can't you?'

The stoat made a small squeak of agreement.

'But that's a job for another day,' Becca continued. 'Right now, I think we should head back home and get dinner started. Hop up on my shoulder.'

'Now you're talking!' said Vinnie.

At that, Cethlenn snapped to attention. She could hear

the sound of whooshing grass as the woman began to trudge back through the field and away from the well. Away from her. She had only a moment to consider before Becca would be too far away for her to follow.

When she took refuge in the well all those years ago, it was because she believed that when the Tuatha Dé Danann left the mortal realm, the last dregs of magic had left with them. She thought her chance at revenge was long gone and that she would stay in this dark hole until time and memory were no more. But the appearance of this young woman complicated matters. She said she was going to come back another day, but that could be weeks away and now that a new world of possibility had opened up for her, Cethlenn found she could no longer wait a single second. Without a backward glance, she surged up through the mouth of the well and began to follow the young woman home.

After so many years rotting in isolation, Cethlenn's mind had begun to whirr back to life and the first thing she thought of was revenge.

CHAPTER ONE

Crosses and Not

'I don't think I'm doing it right,' said Cat, throwing her half-finished St Brigid's Cross down on the coffee table in frustration. 'It's all weird and wonky looking.'

'*You're* weird and wonky looking,' said Shane.

'Oh, ha ha! And I suppose yours is perfect, is it?'

She looked over at Shane who was tying a rubber band over one arm of his own cross, which Cat noticed to her annoyance was indeed perfect looking.

'It's not that hard,' he said, shooting her a self-satisfied grin.

'Well done, Shane,' said Cat's granny, who was hovering over them inspecting their handiwork. 'You must take that home with you and show your mammy and Uncle Brian.'

The sound of pots and pans crashing to the ground grabbed Granny's attention and Cat took the opportunity to mouth *Nerd!* at Shane, who stuck out his tongue in return.

'What's going on in there?' Granny yelled. 'Do I need to come in and clean up your mess?'

A small bald head appeared at the living-room door and looked in at them sheepishly. It had been three months since Cat first met the fairy known as the Clurichaun, but she still felt a little thrill whenever he appeared. It reminded her that the events of Halloween night had really happened, that she had ventured into the world of dangerous and magical creatures and lived to tell the tale. Granny had always told her she had 'The Sight' – the ability to see all things supernatural – but a small part of her had always wondered whether Granny was just trying to make her feel special. When she had woken up on Halloween morning to find that her baby brother Mikey had been taken by the Pooka and the Trooping Fairies and a Changeling had been left in his place, all doubts were gone. She really *did* have The Sight. Ever since then, life hadn't been the same – it seemed as though there was magic everywhere and Cat wanted to learn about it all.

'Nothing to be worrying about, Mrs Donnelly,' said the Clurichaun, sweating slightly and darting his eyes back toward the kitchen. 'I've got it all under control.'

'All right,' said Granny, with some scepticism. 'But call me if you need a hand. The last thing I want is for you to be burning yourself on the hob.'

'Again,' added Cat, under her breath.

The Clurichaun gave a little bob of thanks and scurried back to the kitchen.

Granny sighed, 'What will I do with that fella?'

Another unpleasant surprise Cat had on Halloween morning was learning that Granny was in hospital having suffered a heart attack. She spent a full week recovering and arrived home to find the Clurichaun at her door with cap in hand, looking shamefaced. Apparently, he was feeling guilty over the part he had played in Cat and Shane's Halloween adventure and refused to leave until he made amends. Since Granny wasn't back to full health, she agreed he could help out around the house until she got back on her feet. That was almost three months ago, but the Clurichaun showed no sign of leaving. Granny pretended to be annoyed by it, but she had to admit that having an extra pair of hands around to help with the cooking and cleaning was useful. Plus, Cat knew that they ended each day by sharing a box of biscuits and catching up on that day's soaps. She thought that Granny secretly enjoyed the Clurichaun's company, even if she did complain about him.

'Is this any better?' she asked, holding up her latest lop-sided attempt at cross-making.

Granny tutted, 'All right, budge over and I'll show you how it's done.' She lowered herself to the floor with a small groan and reached for a handful of reeds. 'We'll do one of the three-armed crosses first – they're easier than the four-armed ones to get the hang of. Now, watch my hands.'

Cat watched as Granny began to weave the reeds together, forming a perfect triangle .

'How do you do that so quickly? It has to be magic!' she said, only half joking.

Granny smiled and tied off each arm of the cross with

a rubber band. 'It's no magic, only years of practice. You'll get the hang of it soon, Caitriona.'

'Why are they called St Brigid's *crosses?*' asked Shane, already halfway through weaving his second one, which Cat couldn't help but notice was looking even neater than the last. 'They don't really look like crosses do they? More like ninja throwing stars or something.'

He lobbed the cross at Cat to demonstrate his point.

'What do they be teaching you in school these days?' asked Granny, rolling her eyes. 'They're crosses because the story goes that, hundreds of years ago, St Brigid visited a pagan chieftain who was dying. She was trying to teach him all about Christianity and as she spoke, she picked some pieces of straw off the floor and began to weave them together into this cross shape.'

'Oh,' said Shane, who was clearly a little disappointed in the origin story. 'That's it?'

'Well… no, actually. Brigid is an interesting figure and there's a lot more to her story than that. Run upstairs and grab that notebook of yours, Caitriona. You may want to write this down.'

Cat gave a little squeal of excitement and bounded up

the stairs to her room. In the centre of her desk was a hidden drawer that contained a few small treasures Cat wanted to keep safe, the most important of which was the notebook she had dubbed her 'Book of Secrets'. Her first Book of Secrets was an old copy book covered in Cat's doodles where she would note down all the stories her Granny told her about ghosts and fairies and magic. She had given up that Book of Secrets to the Queen of the Fairies on Halloween night in exchange for her baby brother Mikey's life – something she occasionally thought was a bad deal on those days when Mikey was throwing a tantrum.

When Granny offered to help her make a new Book of Secrets, she decided it should be a bit more special. She found a beautiful hardback notebook with a deep mossy green cover on sale in the newsagents in town and per-suaded her mother to buy it for her.

She had also picked up a gold marker and when she got home had written 'The *NEW* Book of Secrets' on the cover in her best curly handwriting, so it looked suitably important and magical.

Cat grabbed the notebook along with her favourite pen and headed back downstairs to find the Clurichaun had served up some tea and Hobnobs. Cat jammed one of the biscuits in her mouth and opened the notebook to the next blank page. 'Ready!' she said through a mouthful of crumbs.

'All right,' said Granny, settling into her storyteller voice that Cat knew so well. 'Tell me, what do you know about Brigid?'

'She's one of the patron saints of Ireland,' said Shane.

'And?' said Granny.

Cat and Shane looked blankly at Granny. They didn't know much else.

'Lord bless us and save us; they really don't be teaching you much at school! She is indeed one of the three patron saints of Ireland along with St Colmcille and St Patrick, although for my money, she's far more impressive than either of those lads were. Her father was a pagan chieftain and back in those days, daughters were only seen as worthy if they were good marriage material and by that, of course they meant young and beautiful,' said Granny, with a roll of her eyes.

'That isn't fair!' said Cat. 'What do someone's looks

have to do with whether or not they'd be a good wife or husband?'

'You're right, it isn't fair, but her father was a cruel man and that was his way of thinking. In his mind, Brigid needed to be married off to the highest bidder as soon as possible. If he'd had any sense, he would have seen what a brilliant smart girl he had, and he'd have let her make up her own mind about what she wanted to do. For as long as she could remember, Brigid had wanted to be a nun, so she prayed and prayed to make herself as unattractive as possible – and it worked! Every man who came to her father looking to marry Brigid got hit with a sense of unease about the girl and each and every one of them decided that she wasn't the wife for them. Word got around and soon, no man in the country would even darken their door. Eventually, her father gave in and let her go off and become a nun.

'In time, Brigid went on to perform many miracles. You might have learned in school about the time she went to the King of Leinster and asked him for land to build a monastery on. He refused at first, but our Brigid had a plan. She made a deal with him to give her as much land as she could cover with her cloak. The king thought this was very funny indeed and agreed, thinking it would be a bit of fun. Little did he know, Brigid's cloak was magic, and when she spread it out it grew and grew until it covered half the countryside! I don't think he was laughing any more after that.

'Brigid was also a great healer. When I was a girl, everyone would leave a scrap of cloth outside on the eve of St Brigid's Day – an old rag or dishtowel. The story goes that Brigid would bless the cloth as she passed by with the morning dew and then you would take it back inside and use it to cure headaches throughout the year. There's also a holy well dedicated to Brigid not too far from here but I haven't been there myself in many years.'

Cat jotted down notes in The Book of Secrets as Granny spoke, but she couldn't help but feel a little disappointed. So far, everything Granny said sounded like it could have been done by any saint. She couldn't see why Brigid was so special.

'But there's another side to the story that makes Brigid even more interesting and complicated, at least in my eyes,' said Granny, pausing to take a sip of her tea.

Cat perked up. *Now we're getting somewhere*, she thought.

'In ancient times, long before St Patrick brought Christianity to these shores, there was a tribe who lived on this land called the Tuatha Dé Danann, named after their great goddess, Danu. They were a powerful people who were deeply skilled in magic and the old ways, and they've even come to be thought of as gods and goddesses themselves. Their high chieftain was a man called the Dagda – a big strapping man whose powers were associated with the weather, agriculture and fertility. He had several children, one of whom was a daughter who was said to have been born with fire in her hair, and he named her Brigid.

'No one knows for sure who Brigid's mother was, it may have been Danu herself or it may have been another figure called the Morrigan.'

'I've heard of the Morrigan!' said Cat. 'Wasn't she a goddess of war or something?'

Granny nodded. 'She was indeed. She would take the form of a crow and circle the battlefields of ancient Ireland, foretelling the warriors' doom.'

'So she was evil?' asked Shane.

'Lord, no!' said Granny. 'One thing you'll learn about mythology and Irish myths in particular, is that things are rarely black or white. The Morrigan wasn't bad, but neither was she good. She simply was. Anyway, no matter who her mother was, it seems that Brigid took strongly after her father, becoming the goddess of spring, poetry and healing.

'She was born on the pagan festival of Imbolc, which marks the first day of spring. Can ye guess when that is?'

Cat's eyes lit up; she could see where Granny was going with this. 'Is it the first of February?' she asked.

Granny gave her a wink.

'Same as St Brigid's day…' said Shane. 'Wait, so they're same person?'

'Some people think so,' confirmed Granny. 'When Christianity came to Ireland, the Church worked hard to make sure the pagan religion was stamped out and the old gods and goddesses soon passed into myth… but maybe, just maybe, not all of them did. They share a name, both of them are associated with healing and with water, they share a feast day, and they both were fierce protectors of women. But no matter what you believe, the first of February is still a day to celebrate Brigid and all that she stands for.'

'What do you believe, Granny?' asked Cat.

Granny smiled. 'Oh, I believe lots of things. Caitriona. For example, right now I believe that it's high time you were headed home, young Mr Culligan, before that uncle of yours has my head.'

Shane checked his phone and winced. 'Oops, he texted me fifteen minutes ago telling me dinner was almost ready! I better go. See you tomorrow, Cat. Thanks again, Mrs Donnelly.'

'That's "Granny" to you, lad, and don't forget to take your crosses. Tell your uncle to hang them above the door for luck.'

Shane nodded and headed out the door, calling his goodbye into the Clurichaun.

'That reminds me,' said Granny, hauling herself to her feet. 'I better tell the bould Clurichaun to head away before your mam gets home.'

Granny shuffled into the kitchen and Cat picked up another handful of reeds, determined to make the cross right this time if it killed her.

CHAPTER TWO

Of Witches and Familiars

C at had been having a perfectly normal day, right up until the moment a small, furry creature fell from the sky. She and Shane were walking home from school and arguing about whether it would be cooler to be able to fly or to read minds (fly, obviously), when a screech from overhead made her look up just in time to spot something fall from the branches of tree and land right on Shane's head.

For half a second, Cat did nothing, too stunned by the strange turn of events to do anything other than stare in shock. But then Shane came to his senses and began to yell.

'Agh!' he cried as the creature squeaked and scrabbled around his neck. 'Get it off me, get it off me!' The last word came out as almost a sob.

Cat burst out laughing. She knew he would find a way to pay her back later, but she couldn't help herself – it was too ridiculous.

'Oh dear, I'm so sorry!' said a voice Cat didn't recognise. 'This is all my fault. Vinnie – stop messing around and leave the poor boy alone!'

As Cat wiped the tears from her eyes, she watched as the furry little creature jumped from Shane's shoulder and into the waiting arms of a woman she had never seen before. She was short – only a little taller than Cat herself – and had a round, friendly face. Her bright pink hair stood out at all angles, and it looked as though it hadn't seen a hairbrush for months. She wore round wire-framed glasses that made her eyes look huge and owl-like. When she adjusted them, Cat noticed that she wore chunky silver rings with stones of various colours on each finger.

'He didn't hurt you, did he?' asked the woman while the creature writhed around in her arms and let out an angry squeak. 'Oh hush, I didn't ask how *you* were because I know *you* weren't hurt! Honestly, Vinnie, you're such a drama queen.'

'I'm OK … I think,' said Shane, looking dazed and more than a bit dishevelled after his encounter. 'I'm sorry, is that a *rat* you're holding?'

The woman smiled. 'Stoat actually. This is Vinnie – named after Vincent Van Gogh.'

'Like the artist?' said Cat.

Vinnie the stoat puffed up his chest with pride and now that Cat had a better look at him, she couldn't help but notice the small notch missing from his left ear.

Ah, thought Cat. *I guess the name makes sense.*

'And I'm Becca Ryan … ow!'

To Cat's astonishment, Vinnie the stoat leaned over and nipped Becca on the ear.

'All right, Vinnie, point taken. *Dr* Becca Ryan, I should say. I'm not really used to the whole "doctor" bit yet, but Vinnie strongly feels that I should work it into every conversation.'

'You're a doctor?' Cat asked, feeling a little confused. The only doctors she had ever encountered were her friend Ebele's dad, Dr Abara, and the ones she had met in the hospital when Granny was sick, and they all seemed, well, a little more professional than this woman.

Becca laughed and quickly said, 'Oh no, not *that* kind of doctor. I've just recently gotten a PhD in anthropology. It took me so long I was beginning to think I'd never get there.'

'What's anthropology?' asked Shane and Cat was glad he asked because she was wondering the same thing.

'It's the study of human cultures and societies and how they develop,' said Becca.

'So it's like history?'

'History is certainly a part of it. So is archaeology and biology and natural science – what you focus on depends what area of anthropology you're most interested in. My speciality was in folklore, specifically folk remedies.'

'Folk remedies? Do you mean, like, magic?' Cat asked, shooting a hopeful glance at Shane.

'Well... yes and no. It's complicated. If a folk remedy works, a lot of people would say it's just an example of the placebo effect in action – that's where something only works because you *believe* it'll work. But isn't that a kind of magic itself? If you think about it—'

Vinnie the stoat began chirping in Becca's ear and she threw her hands up in apology.

'Sorry, sorry! Vinnie here was warning me that I was about to stray into nerdy territory, and I was in danger of boring you both. I can't help it really, as an academic and a practising witch I could talk about this stuff till the cows come home!'

Cat and Shane stared at each other with wide grins.

'You're a witch?' Cat asked. 'A real one? Like with spells and stuff?'

Becca smiled. 'I am indeed. Just like my mother and her mother before her. I actually come from a long line of witches going all the way back to at least the 1600s. At least, that's as far back as the family tree extends. It could be even longer for all I know! As for spells, that's actually the reason why you were hit in the head by Vinnie here. I'd spotted a nest at the top of this tree and was hoping there were some old eggshells inside. I've been searching for a robin's egg for a spell I've wanted to do for the longest time. Of course, it's entirely the wrong time of year to be looking for this kind of thing, sure it's only just

Imbolc… uh, that's the first day of spring in the Celtic calendar,' Becca said.

'Oh, we know!' Cat replied.

'You do?' said Becca, looking genuinely pleased. 'Brilliant! I love knowing the younger generation hasn't lost touch with some of the older ways.'

'We have a good teacher,' said Cat, thinking of Granny and wondering what she'd make of this strange young woman who spoke about magic and witchcraft so openly.

'Anyway, as I said, I'd spotted this nest and thought maybe I'd be lucky and there'd be some shell scraps left over from last year, so I sent Vinnie up to check. Poor thing must have lost his balance. Speaking of which… any joy, Vinnie?'

Vinnie the stoat squeaked, and Becca frowned.

'Oh well, better luck next time!' she said.

'Sorry,' said Shane. 'Are you … speaking with Vinnie?'

Becca nodded. 'Vinnie here is what you'd call my familiar. Do you know what they are?'

Shane shook his head, but Cat jumped in right away – she had read a lot about witches, but never thought she'd have the chance to meet one in real life and wanted desperately to make a good impression.

'I do,' she said, 'they're like animal companions that help witches out with spells and magic!'

'Exactly right!' Becca said and Cat felt herself beaming with pride. 'I found Vinnie around two years ago when he was just a kit. Or I should say, *we* found *each other*. When a witch meets her familiar there's an instant connection between them. It's hard to explain, but you just know.'

Becca scratched Vinnie under his chin, and he gave her a happy little chirp in return.

'And you can hear him? He's saying actual words to you?' asked Shane, who was looking at Vinnie curiously.

'Absolutely! Not all witches can speak with their familiars, but luckily, I have a particular affinity for animals. Some animals anyway – never had any luck with cats, but maybe they're just being a bit standoffish. Birds on the other hand—'

Vinnie leaned over and gave Becca another nip on the ear. She shook herself. 'Where are my manners at all? Vinnie here is reminding me that I've been yammering away for ages, and I haven't even asked you two your own names yet! You'll have to forgive me, I'm a bit scattered and I tend to ramble on.'

Cat had noticed, but she didn't mind. She was beginning to like this Dr Becca Ryan. She wasn't like any grownup she had ever met, and she loved hearing from someone else who knew about magic. Cat didn't want her to stop.

'I'm Shane,' said Shane, 'and this is Cat. We live in the estate just over the road.'

'Oh well, then that makes us neighbours! I've just moved into number 7. Speaking of which,' Becca said, looking up, 'we'd better get ourselves home. There's rain coming.'

Cat looked up. She didn't see any rain clouds, but maybe this was some other witchy power of Becca's.

The three of them, along with Vinnie the stoat, walked along the road chatting. Cat learned that Becca had moved to the area to do some research into holy wells and how they'd been used to heal various sicknesses over the years.

'There are thousands of wells all over the country, but for some reason this area in particular is absolutely loaded with them.' Becca said. 'But they can be hard to find sometimes. Over the years, people forget about them, and nature does its thing and takes over. I've been using old maps to try and locate them so I can catalogue them for my research.'

'You should speak to my granny,' Cat said. 'She knows loads about this kind of thing! I bet she'd be able to help.'

'I might just do that,' said Becca, stopping at the gate to number 7. 'Well, it's been lovely to meet you both and I hope we get to chat again soon.'

Cat and Shane waved their goodbyes. As she turned to leave, Cat stopped in her tracks. She thought she saw a strange shadow hovering near Becca's head. A cold sense of dread crept down her spine and she felt her mouth turn dry. She couldn't explain it, but something was wrong; it was as though the energy in the air had shifted. She almost cried out in warning, but by then Becca had opened her front door and disappeared inside.

'Everything all right, Cat?' asked Shane. He was giving her a funny look.

Cat looked back at the door to Becca's house, but there was nothing there. She must have been imagining things.

'Yeah, everything's fine.'

Just then, the sky darkened, and the first drops of rain began to fall. Cat let out a squeal as she and Shane ran the rest of the way home.

The shadow watched them with interest before it slipped back through the door of number 7.

CHAPTER THREE

Unwelcome News

'Hi, Granny, I'm home!' Cat called out as she entered the front door. She flung her schoolbag down in the hallway and hurried into the kitchen, eager to fill Granny in on her day. 'I've got *loads* to tell you – we have a new neighbour and she's a witch and her familiar is a stoat called Vinnie who's missing part of his ear. He fell on Shane's head and—'

Cat cut off when she saw that Granny wasn't alone. Her mother was already home and the two of them were sitting around the kitchen table having tea. Cat felt a momentary stab of panic – her mother was never home from work this early. Had something happened to Mikey or to Auntie Eileen? She braced herself for bad news. But her mother simply smiled at her and said, 'Hi Kitty-Cat! Surprise! I took a half day off work today and thought we could do something nice together this afternoon. Maybe head into town or something?'

Relief washed over Cat. Everything was fine.

'Cool!' she said. 'What are we going to do? Is Granny coming too? What about Mikey?'

'I thought it could be just you and me today,' her mother said. 'Granny's agreed to pick Mikey up from the childminder and babysit for a few hours so we can go and get something nice for dinner. What do you think?'

'Can we go to the place with the hot dogs and chilli cheese chips?' Cat asked.

'Wherever you like!'

Cat bounced up and down on her toes in excitement. She couldn't remember a time she and her mother had gone out and eaten dinner alone together. They normally ate at home – either something made by Granny (or, lately, by the Clurichaun) or else they'd grab a takeaway on a Friday night. This was special.

'Go on upstairs and change out of that school uniform,' said Granny. A little stiffly, Cat thought. Was she upset at being left behind? Cat didn't think so. Granny wasn't a fan of eating 'burgers the size of your head' (her own words) and she thought it was sacrilegious to have a milkshake with dinner. But still, something seemed off.

Cat was still puzzling over it as she made her way upstairs. She was about to head into her room when suddenly, the door to the hot press opened a crack and a familiar face popped out.

'Psst!' whispered the Clurichaun. 'Is your mammy still downstairs?'

'She is,' said Cat. 'Um, why are you hiding up here?'

The Clurichaun gave an exaggerated roll of his eyes and Cat could tell he was about to launch into one of his woe-is-me speeches.

'I was just getting ready to make the dinner. I've a new recipe I want to try by your man Jamie Oliver; you know, the English fella?'

Cat nodded.

'Well, I had only just gotten me onions peeled when who should come marching in the door only your mammy! I took one look at Mary and hoofed it up here to hide until she was gone, only they've been down there for an hour arguing back and forth and now the dinner will be ruined because there won't be enough time to get the onions all caramelly and—'

'Hold on,' Cat interrupted. 'Mam and Granny were fighting? What about?'

'Ah, I dunno,' said the Clurichaun with a dismissive wave. 'Something about whether or not it was the best way to tell you something.'

Cat felt her heart sink again. She had been right to worry: something was definitely going on. Why else would her mother take a half day like that? She had been foolish to think that it was just to surprise her.

'What are they going to tell me?' she asked, part of her dreading the answer.

'I don't know,' snapped the Clurichaun. 'I was too busy hiding in a cupboard and worrying about the lovely dinner I had planned.'

'Well, you won't have to worry for much longer,' Cat said. 'Mam is taking me out for dinner.'

Instead of the relief she anticipated, the Clurichaun looked even more annoyed. 'Oh, so my cooking's not good enough for you now, is it?'

'You ready yet, Cat?' her mother yelled from downstairs.

'Just a second!' Cat called back. She said goodbye to the Clurichaun, who was still muttering about the lack of gratitude and quickly changed into a pair of leggings and a hoodie.

'All right, enjoy yourselves. I'll see ye back here later.' said Granny when Cat came back downstairs. She still looked a little grumpy, Cat thought and she felt the gnawing fear in her belly begin to grow. What could have made her so annoyed?

'Thanks, Mam,' her mother said, grabbing her keys off the hook. 'OK Kitty-Cat – let's go!'

Granny looked as though she was about to say something, but instead she shook her head and closed the door behind them.

* * *

Despite her worry about what was going on between Granny and her mother, Cat soon found that she was having a great time. She had been allowed to pick the radio station on the drive into town – a rare treat – and her mother didn't complain even once about how bad the music was or how annoyed she was by the DJ's voice. Once in town, they headed straight for the shops. She hadn't been too excited about that at first (Cat found clothes shopping boring and having to try on endless jumpers and jeans made her feel hot and itchy), but she had to admit, the stuff they had picked out for her in Penneys was actually pretty cool. She couldn't wait to show her friends, Ebele and the twins.

After they had their fill of the clothes shops, they stopped into the bookshop and her mother let her pick out two books. One was a kind of murder mystery set at a boarding school and the other was one of her mother's favourites when she was younger.

'You'll love it, Kitty-Cat,' she said, staring at the cover with a nostalgic look. Cat thought it looked a bit babyish for her, but she didn't want to ruin the moment, so she just smiled and said thanks.

Finally, they headed for the American-style diner Cat had begged her mother to take her to and settled themselves into one of their squeaky red vinyl booths. Cat ordered a hot dog, curly fries and a strawberry milkshake, while her mother asked for a Caesar salad with dressing on the side. Cat could never understand why someone would order a salad for dinner when they could have chips, but each to their own.

They were halfway through dinner when Cat noticed her mother wasn't eating her food, just pushing it around on her plate.

'Is your salad bad? You can have some of my chips if you like,' she said, feeling generous of spirit.

'What?' said her mother, seeming to snap out of her daze. 'Oh no, thanks, love. This is fine. I'm not really hungry.'

Cat shrugged. More for her!

'Cat,' said her mother slowly. 'You had a good time this evening, yeah?'

Cat nodded enthusiastically. 'It's been brilliant,' she said, but her mouth was so stuffed full of hot dog it came out a bit muffled.

'Good, that's good. I wanted to make sure you know how much I love you and that you'll always be my special girl.'

Cat swallowed. Suddenly she remembered her conversation with the Clurichaun, which, in the excitement of her afternoon, she had all but forgotten about.

They were fighting about the best way to tell me something.

Was this it? Was this the moment she was going to find out what was going on. Cat looked at the bright pink drink in front of her and suddenly felt sick.

'I want you to know that no matter what happens, you and Mikey are my number one priority,' her mother continued. 'Being with the two of you is the best part of my day and I'm so glad I'm your mam.'

Cat could feel her heart beating faster and faster in her chest. Something was wrong. Was Granny sick? Was *she* sick? She couldn't stand it any more.

'Mam what's wrong, please just tell me!' she said, afraid if she waited any longer she'd burst.

'Nothing's wrong! I'm sorry, Cat, I just—' she took a deep breath and Cat realised she was nervous about something. 'I don't know the best way to talk to you about this but… you know how, ever since your dad and I split up, I've been on my own?'

Cat nodded, feeling confused. Where was she going

with this?

'And I was fine with that – as I said, you and Mikey are my world and that's all I need. But recently... well, recently I made a new friend. His name is Darren.'

Cat felt the bottom drop out of her stomach.

'He's nice and smart and very funny. He works in IT so he's really into computers and stuff...'

Her mother kept talking but the words faded out until all Cat could hear was a buzzing sound like a broken radio. It was all so clear to her now.

'Is he your *boyfriend*?' she blurted out, not making any effort to hide her disgust at the word. Her mother was too old to have a boyfriend. It was gross and weird. Her mother's face turned a shade of bright red and that was all the answer Cat needed.

'I think you'll really like him once you get to know him, Kitty-Cat. And he actually has a daughter around your age too so maybe—'

Cat stood up abruptly, knocking into the table and causing the milkshake to slosh over the glass. 'I want to go home now,' she said.

'Are you sure? You haven't finished your dinner.'

'I said I want to go home!' Cat could hear how whiny she sounded, but she didn't care. So this was what Granny and her mother had been arguing over – how best to tell her the news. But did either of them consider that maybe she didn't want to know this at all?

'Cat, please…' Her mother's voice was all wobbly and Cat could see she was upset. Good. Cat was upset too. You don't just spring boyfriends on people and expect them to be OK with it.

They sat in silence for the whole drive home. They didn't even turn on the radio this time. Once or twice her mother would try and say something to her, but Cat was having none of it. She just sat with her arms crossed, looking out the window. She was angry, there was no doubt, but there was another feeling too – a small seed of fear that took root in her belly. What was going to happen now? Was she about to lose her mother to this Darren guy? Things were changing and Cat wasn't ready.

When they pulled up at the house, she jumped out of the car without offering to help her mother with the shopping bags. She opened the front door and marched straight into the living room where she found Granny bouncing Mikey on her hip while he watched a cartoon.

'Home already?' Granny asked, raising an eyebrow in surprise.

'Did you know?'

Granny's face fell and that told Cat everything she needed to know

'Caitriona, your mammy…'

'Why didn't you tell me?' Cat asked, cutting her off. She didn't wait for Granny's response. It didn't matter what Granny might say to defend herself, the betrayal Cat felt was too much. She turned on her heels and stormed upstairs, past her mother who was struggling in the door with the bags of clothes and books she'd bought her. Bribery, Cat now realised. Something to soften the blow. She didn't want any of those things any more. They were ruined now.

'Cat, wait!' her mother called.

Cat just had time to hear Granny say, 'Leave her be, Laura, she just needs some time' before she slammed her bedroom door shut and threw herself down on her bed and began to cry.

CHAPTER FOUR

Tea and Tarot

The next day, Cat got up and got ready for school without saying a single word to her mother.

'Do you want some juice, Kitty-Cat?' she had asked when Cat first walked into the kitchen, but Cat simply ignored her. Her mother looked upset when Cat sat down at the kitchen table and began shovelling down a bowl of Corn Flakes as quickly as she could. Cat felt a small twinge of guilt at that, but she couldn't help herself. She had just found out the people she loved most in the world had been keeping a giant secret from her. Didn't she have a right to be hurt too?

She had lain awake for hours the night before, replaying the last few weeks over and over again in her mind. Should she have seen this coming somehow? She hadn't noticed anything unusual at the time, but the more she thought about it, she realised that there had indeed been a few nights recently where her mother had come home late. On those nights, Granny was always there to mind her and Mikey; Cat was so absorbed in listening to Granny's stories and working on her Book of Secrets, she hadn't thought twice about where her mother was. Now she knew.

'Have a good day at school, love,' Mam called as Cat slung her schoolbag over her shoulder and headed out the door. She almost said something then. Almost asked one of the many questions that were bubbling around in her brain. But she didn't. She wasn't ready to speak to her mother just yet.

Things weren't much better for Cat at school. Her friends could see that she was mad about something, but when she told them all about it at eleven o'clock break she didn't get quite the response she expected.

'So your mam has a boyfriend,' said Sarah. 'Why is that a problem?'

Cat was dumbfounded. 'You don't think it's completely unfair?' she asked.

'Why?' added Sarah's twin sister Jess. 'Like what's unfair about it?'

Of course, they wouldn't understand. Cat thought. *Their parents are still together. They have no idea what it's like.*

She turned to her two best friends, Shane and Ebele, sure that at least one of them would offer some words of sympathy. Ebele just shrugged and mouthed the word 'sorry' at her. She clearly agreed with the others that it wasn't a big deal.

Shane, looking somewhat uncomfortable, said, 'Isn't it a good thing if it makes her happy?'

'My dad has a girlfriend,' Karol added, unhelpfully. 'She's nice.'

Cat could feel herself turning red with anger. So that was it. She really was alone here.

'You don't get it,' she said. 'None of you do.'

Finding out her mother had a boyfriend felt like a betrayal. As though the life they had wasn't enough for her. As though *she* wasn't enough for her. And it hurt. For so long Cat and her mother had been a team – the two of them against the world. When Mikey came along, it stung to know that she wasn't her mother's only priority any more, but at least Mikey was *family*. Who was this Darren guy? A stranger. A stranger who was taking her mother away from her.

The sound of the bell summoned them back to class, but Cat's anger didn't abate. She stewed in her own rage all throughout their maths lesson and when lunchtime rolled around, she ate her sandwich in silence and refused to speak to any of her friends. When the final bell rang at the end of the day, Cat shot up from her seat and hurried ahead, ignoring the shouts of her friends for her to wait for them.

'Leave her be,' she could hear Shane say and she felt absurdly grateful. He might not understand why she was so mad, but at least he realised how important it was for her to be left alone right now.

She walked through town under her own personal storm cloud of misery, so lost in her own thoughts that she was almost at the estate before she remembered that Granny would be at her house. Granny, who had known all about her mother and Darren. Granny who hadn't told her. Hadn't warned her. Suddenly, Cat realised that she wasn't ready to face Granny either. With so many people to avoid, she felt at a complete loss for what to do next. She stood still, feeling the chill of the February breeze ruffle her hair, and felt her face grow hot as her eyes filled with tears.

Suddenly, a figure appeared before her. Through her tears, she could make out a familiar halo of pink hair and she realised it was Becca.

'Hello, Cat!' said Becca, her voice cheery. 'Where's your partner in crime today?'

'Oh, um, he's not here,' said Cat lamely as she wiped her eyes with the back of her sleeve. She didn't want to explain that she wasn't speaking to Shane – or anyone – right now. Once she could make her out clearly, Cat saw that Vinnie was once again perched on Becca's shoulder and she gave the stoat a small wave.

Becca's smile turned into a frown as she looked Cat over.

'Everything OK?' she asked. 'You seem a bit out of sorts.'

Cat thought about lying and saying she was fine, but

the anger that had sustained her since the night before had fizzled away and she was just so tired and lonely. To her embarrassment, Cat found herself bursting into tears.

Becca looked alarmed. 'Oh no, I'm sorry! I didn't mean to upset you.' She began rummaging through her pockets, finally pulling out a dubious-looking tissue and offering it to Cat. 'It's clean, I swear!' said Becca. Cat took the tissue and blew her nose.

'Do you want me to walk you home?'

Cat shook her head and explained through deep gulping sobs that she didn't want to go home just yet. She began to tell Becca the whole story, who looked on with sympathy.

'Well look, we can't have you wandering around the estate in this weather. Come inside and we'll have a cup of tea and one of the scones I baked this morning. They're a bit burnt in places – completely forgot to set the timer – but you can scrape those bits off and sure, with enough jam who'd even notice?'

Cat hesitated for a second. She didn't really know Becca, but she seemed so nice, and she was the only person so far who hadn't told Cat she was overreacting about Darren, so she wiped away her tears and nodded.

'Lovely!' said Becca, clapping her hands together. 'You'll have to forgive the mess. I'm still moving in and there are boxes everywhere.'

They made the short walk to number 7, Becca talking all the while about the state of her living room. Cat felt soothed. It was nice to have a break from her own thoughts and just listen to someone else for a while. When they reached the house, Becca unlocked the door and went in first. Cat was about to follow, but the second she stepped over the threshold, she was filled with a sudden feeling of dread. It was the same feeling as yesterday – as though there was something there, something powerful and dangerous, and it was watching her. The whole world began to spin before her eyes and Cat reached for the wall to steady herself.

'Are you OK, Cat?' asked Becca. 'You almost fell over!'

For a split second, Cat thought she saw the same dark shadow she'd seen the day before hovering over Becca's shoulder. She almost cried out, but in the blink of an eye it was gone and there was just Becca looking at her through her thick owlish glasses, her face full of concern.

'I... I'm fine,' Cat said, but she wasn't really. She couldn't put her finger on it, but something still felt off.

'Are you sure? You look like you've seen a ghost.'

'Yeah, honestly, I'm just a bit dizzy.'

Vinnie began bobbing up and down excitedly and squeaking in Becca's ear. She frowned.

'Maybe you're right after all,' she said to the stoat before turning to Cat and translating. 'Vinnie here has been telling me all week that there's something strange going on in this house. I haven't felt anything unusual, but animals and children are often more attuned to these things so maybe I'm just getting old.'

Becca smiled and Cat felt herself smiling back. The feeling of dread had eased, and she was already starting to feel better.

'I'll burn some sage later to cleanse the place,' said Becca. 'In the meantime, come in and make yourself at home. Living room's through there.'

Cat stepped into the hallway and the sensations of the last few minutes were completely forgotten as she took in the sight before her. It was a mess, that much was true. Giant black bags stuffed with towels and sheets lined the narrow front hall along with boxes with words like 'Kitchen stuff' and 'Fragile: Glass' written on them in black ink. But despite the mess, Cat found the house completely captivating. The walls were all painted a cheery butter-yellow and there were plants in every corner – fresh green ones poking out of colourful pots and bunches of lavender and sage hung upside down to dry.

The living room contained a large, squishy looking couch covered in knitted blankets and throws and a coffee table strewn with thick waxy candles and crystals of varying sizes that seemed to hum with a quiet magic. There was also a deck of cards with strange designs Cat had never seen before. She was examining them when Becca appeared with two mugs of tea in one hand and a plate piled high with semi-burned scones in the other.

'There we are now,' she said, setting the burden down on the coffee table and shoving her various magical knick-knacks out of the way to make room. She broke a scone in half for Vinnie who hopped off her shoulder and began happily digging in.

'What are these?' asked Cat, holding up the deck of cards.

'That's my tarot deck,' replied Becca. 'Well, one of them anyway. I have about six decks knocking around. Have you ever seen tarot cards before?'

Cat shook her head.

'I use them when I need guidance on something. Each of the cards have a different meaning and you can use them to help you work through any issues you might have. Sometimes you'll take three cards and place them on a table to symbolise what's going on in your past, present, future, but you can also just pull a single card if you want some quick answers. Here, let me show you.'

Cat handed over the deck and watched as Becca closed her eyes and shuffled the cards in her hands. Finally, she held them out to Cat.

'Pick one,' she said. 'The first card that calls to you.'

Cat hesitated. She wasn't entirely sure what that meant. But she reached out and ran her fingers over the partially spread deck until she felt it. A small tug that reminded her of the feeling she got when she was using The Sight. This was the card for her.

Becca nodded. 'Now turn it over.'

Cat flipped the card over. Face up, it showed a picture

of a woman standing in the woods at night. All around her, strange symbols were drawn and above her head a small sliver of a crescent moon was visible.

'What does this card mean?' she asked.

'That's *The Moon*,' replied Becca. 'It can mean a lot of things depending on how you interpret it. It could mean that you're worried or confused about something. Or it could be a warning that you're entering a time of deception and illusion and you need to be aware of what's going on around you as best you can so you can try to find your way back.'

'Oh,' said Cat. 'That doesn't sound good.'

'Don't worry, there's no such thing as a bad card. The tarot is just a tool to help guide you. But um, maybe keep your wits about you for a few days,' said Becca with a wink.

Cat looked down at the card, thoughtfully. 'You really are a witch,' she said.

'I am indeed,' Becca confirmed. 'But anyone can learn to read the tarot.'

'Would you teach me? Someday, I mean,' Cat asked with a hopeful flutter in her chest. She loved learning from Granny, but the things Becca knew were totally different and she wanted to soak in as much knowledge about magic as she could.

'I'd be delighted.'

Cat smiled and bit into her scone and tried to look as though she was enjoying it (it really was quite burned on the bottom).

'What about spells?' Cat said. 'When we met you yesterday, you said you were looking for a spell ingredient. How do those work?'

'Well, for one thing, the spells I do might not look much like you expect. I can't make things appear in a puff of smoke or anything like that. But much like the tarot, I use spells to help guide me or sometimes to help me manifest things that I want in life. For example, in my current research into holy wells I've been able to do some spells that help me hone in on the right energy I'm looking for and...' she stopped suddenly and eyed Cat. 'You must think I'm completely mad. All this talk of magic and stuff.'

Cat shook her head. 'No, I totally believe you. In fact...' she bit her lip. She wanted to tell this woman all about her own abilities, the way she could sense the supernatural through her use of The Sight, about the adventures she'd had last Halloween when she and Shane had faced down the Queen of the Fairies and the creature known as the Pooka to save their siblings. She had never spoken about these things with anyone other than Shane and her Granny, but she liked Becca. She trusted her and wanted so desperately for Becca to like her in return. So she told her.

At the end of her tale, Becca sat back looking stunned and Cat was worried she had said too much. But suddenly Becca let out a loud whoop of laughter. 'I knew I moved here for a reason! Absolutely teeming with magic and knowledge of the old ways. Now, tell me more about your Book of Secrets.'

Cat was so absorbed in her conversation that she didn't notice a shadow slink into the room. Nor did she notice it lean in closer as if it were listening too.

CHAPTER FIVE

Good Days

Shane didn't like leaving Cat when she was in that kind of mood, but when he saw her storm off at the end of the day, he knew she needed some time alone to cool off.

'Cat! Wait up!' called Ebele, racing to try and catch up to her, but Shane put a hand on her shoulder and shook his head.

'Leave her be,' he said. 'She just needs to calm down a bit. Things will be better tomorrow.'

'I don't get what's wrong with her,' Jess said, as they walked in a group out of the school gate toward home.

'Yeah, it's not like Cat at all,' said Sarah.

'Are you sure we shouldn't follow her, just to see if she's OK?' asked Ebele.

'I don't know,' said Karol. 'When I'm mad, I don't really want to be around anyone.'

'When are you ever mad?' said Sarah with a laugh that they all joined in with. Karol was the quietest boy in class and none of them had ever heard him so much as raise his voice in the year and half he had lived in Clonbridge.

Karol just smiled and shrugged his shoulders.

They continued to walk and talk, and Shane let it all wash over him. He still couldn't quite believe he had this group of friends – people who actually wanted to be around him, who laughed and joked and had fun with him. He had even stayed over at Karol's house last weekend, and they had stayed up all night playing games on the PlayStation and eating sour jellies until his stomach hurt and his tongue felt raw from the sugar. He hadn't minded though. It had felt so good, so normal. Shane had been alone for so long, he had almost forgotten what it was like to just have fun.

Ever since his father died two years ago, Shane had felt responsible for minding his little sister Jenny and for helping to keep his mother together on days when she would rather fall apart. But a few weeks before Christmas, things had changed. Shane's uncle Brian and his husband Greg called in for a visit unexpectedly. They were at a friend's wedding in a nearby hotel and thought it might be nice to pop in and see the family for the afternoon. It just so happened that their visit coincided with one of his mother's bad days. Actually, it had been a string of bad days in a row by then, and Brian and Greg were shocked to see how difficult things had gotten. Shane still remembered Brian's eyes filling with tears as he hugged him close and promised him he wouldn't be alone any more.

To Shane's delight, his uncle was true to his word. Brian and Greg figured out a system where Brian would split his time between Shane's house and their own house up in Bray. He worked for himself as a graphic designer and said he could just as easily work from the kitchen table as his desk. So that's what he did. Every week he would spend five nights with Shane and his family, helping around the house and making dinner every night, before returning home for the weekend to be with Greg.

At first, Shane worried that the arrangement wouldn't

work. His mother had always been a private person and he didn't think she would want her younger brother fussing over her. But under Brian's care, she started to slowly come back out of her shell. Things were better for Shane too – having someone around who he could talk to about his problems made the burden seem a lot lighter.

He actually looked forward to coming home from school now that there were more good days than bad. He loved opening the front door to find Brian and Jenny performing one of their choreographed dance routines as his mother laughed and clapped along. It was good to have the house filled with happiness again.

That's why Shane couldn't understand why Cat was so mad at her mother for getting a boyfriend. Shouldn't she want her mother to be happy? Now that Shane had the warmth of his own mother's smile back in his life again, he would do just about anything to keep it there.

When Sarah and Jess suggested they all go over to their house for a while, Shane took out his phone and texted Brian asking if it was OK.

'Absolutely!' came the response, 'Enjoy yourself.'

Shane smiled. His mother was doing better, and he

finally had a real group of friends. Life was good.

And Cat will come around, he thought. *She always does in the end.*

CHAPTER SIX

An Opportunity Arises

I t had been several days since Cethlenn followed the witch home from the well and still no opportunity had presented itself. She had tried whispering thoughts into her ear as she slept, tried using her power to influence the witch in subtle ways, but it was no use. Becca seemed completely oblivious to her presence. The little creature who was always trailing the witch did seem to sense her every now and again and Cethlenn spent a few hours entertaining herself by occasionally running an invisible hand over the stoat's back and watching its fur bristle.

'I'm telling you, Becca, there's something here,' it said, its small beady eyes darting around the room. It was clearly scared, and this pleased Cethlenn. It wasn't much, scaring a mere stoat, but it had been so long since any creature had feared her. She missed it – the power that came with fear.

'Don't be silly, Vinnie,' replied the witch. These houses are no more than twenty years old. There are no spirits floating around. Believe me, I'd know if there was.'

The young woman was so filled with pride, so sure of her abilities. Foolish.

Or perhaps it was Cethlenn who was the foolish one? Did she really think that after so long she had finally found someone who could aid her in getting her revenge? Perhaps she should just return to the well and to her solitude.

She was considering giving up when she met the girl. Though she was just a child, Cethlenn could feel the power that lay within her. Her magic wasn't fully formed, not yet, but it had the potential to be strong. For a brief moment, the girl had sensed her too, Cethlenn was sure of it. But she had been sure of things before and that had led to her downfall. This time, she would be patient. Next time she saw the girl, she would test her.

Her opportunity came sooner than she anticipated. The very next day, Becca arrived home with the girl in tow and Cethlenn decided to push her awareness, just a little bit. She reached deep into her power which had lain dormant for so long and allowed her presence to grow stronger. It worked! The girl had recoiled the second she crossed the threshold. Cethlenn could be sure now: the girl was a true sensitive.

Cethlenn allowed her presence to fade, allowed the girl to settle down and to feel safe again, while Cethlenn watched and listened.

Cethlenn listened with interest as the girl opened up to the witch about her ability. 'The Sight' she called it. She listened as the girl spoke of her adventures last Samhain and Cethlenn marvelled at names she hadn't heard in hundreds of years – the Merrow, the Dullahan, the *Sídhe*. The girl was the one she needed; she knew it. As Becca and Cat chatted, Cethlenn's mind turned to scheming.

Suddenly the girl stood up.

'Thanks for the scones and … for listening.'

'Anytime,' said the witch. The girl was leaving and so Cethlenn did something she had not done since she was a foolish girl herself. She panicked. She couldn't let this opportunity slip away. What she was about to do was risky. There was a chance after so many years that she wasn't strong enough, but she had to try...

As the front door opened and the girl turned to wave goodbye, Cethlenn acted. She summoned all her will, whatever strength was left in her, and threw herself into the body of the witch, forcing the young woman's spirit out. For the first time in a millennium, Cethlenn looked out at the world through a pair of mortal eyes.

'Stop!' she cried out, causing the girl to spin around in surprise.

Too loud, Cethlenn thought and tried to remember what it was like to speak as a creature made of flesh and bone.

'Must you depart so soon?' she added, making an effort to sound meek, like a mortal would. To Cethlenn's annoyance, the girl seemed confused by her question. She felt the rage begin to build, but forced herself to remain calm. She needed the girl, however much she wished it were otherwise.

What would the witch say? she thought. 'What I mean

to say is, won't you stay awhile? I can… make us more tea.' Her tongue tripped over unfamiliar teeth, and she forced her mouth into a grin.

Cethlenn saw the girl hesitate. She didn't want to go home; she had said so herself. And if she could just keep her here a bit longer…

'I have been thinking about your little problem,' said Cethlenn. 'And I think I know of a way for you to solve it.'

Cat looked at Becca curiously.

'My … problem?'

'Your mother and her…boyfriend.' Cethlenn choked on the word. What embarrassing creatures these mortals are.

Cat swallowed. 'Oh yeah, *that* problem.'

'What if I told you there may be a way to make it all go away?'

She had the girl's attention now.

'How do you mean?'

'Take a seat and I shall tell you all about it.'

Cat sat back down and Cethlenn went into the kitchen to collect her thoughts. She gripped the edge of the countertop and took a deep breath, forcing herself to hold onto the body she now occupied. All the while, she could sense the spirit of the witch, beating against her defences, trying with all her might to get back in.

Her concentration was broken by the squeak of the stoat, who had appeared at the door and was peering up at her curiously.

'Becca?' he asked with a tremor in his voice. 'What's going on? You don't smell right. You almost smell like...'

Cethlenn turned and glared down at the creature and his fur stood on end. As soon as she locked eyes with him the stoat began to panic and squeal. She reached down and grabbed him by the scruff of the neck, ignoring the bites and scratches on her hands as he thrashed around – it was good to feel pain again, to feel anything again. She opened the back door, flung the creature out into the garden, and slammed the door shut again. She could hear his tiny claws scratching against the white plastic, trying desperately to get back in. She ignored the sound and made a fist, forcing her will as hard as she could against the spirit of the witch who was still fighting her, still trying to get back into her own body. She took a breath. She didn't know how long she could stay in this body, so it was time to seize her opportunity.

CHAPTER SEVEN

The *Geas*

Cat felt exhausted but strangely elated. She had spent the past hour chatting with Becca about all manner of things, from her ability with The Sight to the fight she'd had with her mother the night before. To her surprise and delight, Becca didn't once tell her that she was overreacting about Darren. She just nodded sympathetically and told Cat she understood. It was so nice to have someone just listen to her. Becca had also shown her a few more things – as well as her tarot cards, she had a seemingly endless collection of books and magical talismans from around the world. By the time she stood to leave, Cat's head was practically swimming in the sea of magical energy all around her.

She had been saying her goodbyes, when something strange happened. Out of nowhere, Becca became insistent that she stay longer. Cat knew she needed to go home, it was getting close to dinner time and Granny would be worried about her, but when Becca mentioned something about a magical solution to her current problem, she knew she couldn't leave just yet.

What's the harm in hearing her out? Cat thought.

She sat back down and waited for Becca to come back from the kitchen.

She was just bending over to examine a particularly interesting-looking crystal on the coffee table when a series of high-pitched squeaks – followed by the sound of the door slamming – drew her attention.

'Becca?' she called. 'Is everything OK?'

When she didn't get an answer, Cat made her way to the kitchen. She found Becca bent over the sink, her hands gripping the counter tightly.

'Becca?' she said again.

Becca turned, and for a split second, Cat's vision blurred, and it seemed to her as though there were two

women standing before her, the Becca she knew and...
someone else. Someone wreathed in shadow. In the blink
of an eye the vision was gone and there was just Becca,
looking pinched and worn.

'The tea's almost ready,' said Becca, and Cat thought
her voice sounded strained.

She looked around the kitchen and noticed there was
no sign of the stoat. 'Where's Vinnie?' she asked. 'I could
hear him squealing and—'

'The stoat is fine,' Becca said, cutting Cat off. 'He
needed some air, so I let him out. Shall we go back to the
living room?'

Cat hesitated; something wasn't right. Becca had been
so friendly and jolly this afternoon but now she suddenly
she seemed cold. Maybe it was time for her to go after
all...

As though she had just read Cat's thoughts, Becca
broke into a smile. 'I found some cake to go with the
tea. Don't worry. I didn't bake this one.' She held up a
box from the local bakery and Cat felt her mouth water.
Becca's scones had been pretty dismal, but she knew for
a fact that O'Connell's made an *excellent* chocolate fudge

cake.

They settled themselves back in the living room and Cat began tucking into the cake. She didn't care that she had probably ruined her appetite for dinner – it was worth it.

'Now,' said Becca, placing her cup down and looking Cat squarely in the eyes. 'On to the problem at hand. Your mother is in love with this Darren person and that upsets you, correct?'

Cat hesitated. That was true, but hearing it laid out so bluntly made her feel a bit strange. Finally, she nodded.

'And you wish for things to go back to the way they were before?'

Again, Cat didn't know quite what to say to that. She did want that, with all her heart, but a little part of her knew how selfish that sounded. She didn't want Becca to think less of her for it.

'Well?' Becca pressed.

'Yes,' Cat said. 'Things were fine before. I don't know why they have to change.'

Becca smiled and the pain Cat felt in her stomach began to die down. Maybe she wasn't a bad person for wishing this after all?

'As I said, there may be a way for you to change your mother's mind. To make her forget she ever knew Darren… Tell me, Cat, have you ever heard of the Dagda?'

'Yeah!' she replied, pleased she could show Becca how much she knew. 'He was one of the leaders of the Tuatha Dé Danann – they were, like, gods of ancient Ireland. My Granny told me about them.'

'Of course she did,' said Becca, and Cat thought she looked oddly irritated. 'But did she also tell you that the Tuatha Dé Danann were invaders? That they stole this land from its rightful owners?'

Cat raised her eyebrows in surprise. Now this was something new.

Becca nodded. 'It's true. There were other folk who lived here long before the coming of the Tuatha Dé Danann. When they arrived on these shores, they did as all conquering forces do – they swept through the land, consolidating their power and killing all those who would oppose them. Their leader, as you know, was the Dagda, a large bumbling oaf of a man if ever there was one. The source of his power and authority came from his possession of three great treasures.

'The first of these treasures was a cauldron called *Coire Ansic*, which never grew empty, thus allowing him to feed a whole army for months on end. The second was a magical staff called *Lorg Mór* that was so strong it could kill nine people in a single stroke and, when wielded by the Dagda, was said to hold the power to bring people back from the dead. The third treasure was *Uaithne*, a hand-held harp made of carved oak. Some said that the music of *Uaithne* was so powerful it could change the seasons. But it also had another use: *Uaithne* could change people's emotions and shape their thoughts. At the sound of *Uaithne*'s music, laughter would turn to tears and anger would give way to calm. These were powerful items, I think you'll agree, and when the Dagda had possession of them, no one could stand in his or his people's way.

'The Tuatha Dé Danann fought many battles in their time, but perhaps the most famous – or most infamous – was the Second Battle of Moytura where they faced off against their deadliest foes – the Fomorians.'

Cat was fascinated, she had never heard of the Dagda's treasures or the Fomorians before. She wished she had her Book of Secrets with her so she could take some notes.

'History depicts the Fomorians as monstrous beings,' Becca continued with a sneer. 'Giants or ogres or even pirates, they say! But none of that is true. The Fomorians are – were – a noble race of people. At that time, their leader was a man called Balor. Now *there* was a hero. He was brave and strong and wise. His enemies dubbed him "Balor of the Evil Eye", and for good reason. When Balor was a young man, he witnessed a group of druids conducting a death spell and as he watched, the fumes entered his eye and left him with the power of destruction. Whoever he turned his gaze on would fall dead instantly.

'Balor had a wife whom he loved more than all the stars in the sky. She was a warrior too, his equal in every way. Her … her name was Cethlenn.'

Becca paused, taking a deep breath in and Cat was surprised to find that her new friend's eyes were shiny with tears. In the silence that sat between them, Cat could just make out the sound of scraping coming from the back door. She was about to ask whether she should let Vinnie back in, when Becca picked up her story again.

'Cethlenn received a prophecy that Balor would one day die at the hands of his own grandson, so she and Balor did what they must to prevent the prophecy from coming to pass. They locked their only daughter, Eithne, away in a tower so no one would fall in love and sire a child with her.

'Despite their best efforts, Eithne did manage to fall in love, with a member of the Tuatha Dé Danann of all people! Together, they had a child, a son they named Lugh, who they managed to keep secret for many long years. When Balor found out, he went wild with rage and ordered the child to be killed, but Lugh escaped and went to live with the enemy.

'The Tuatha Dé Danann and the Fomorians had many reasons to despise each other, and this was but one more insult Balor had to face. When they met on the fields of Moytura that fateful day, they were primed for battle, and everyone knew that only one side would emerge victorious. The Tuatha Dé Danann were confident it would be them – for how could anyone stand against them when they had the treasures of the Dagda at their beck and call?

'But the Fomorians had a plan to turn the tides of the

conflict in their favour. While the battle raged on, a small band of brave Fomorian warriors slipped away unnoticed. They infiltrated the Dagda's fortress at a place called Brú na Bóinne and stole away his magic harp, so that he could no longer use it to give strength to his tired soldiers or to fill their hearts with a killing rage. They brought the harp back to their own stronghold, sure that victory would soon be theirs and their fellow Fomorians would return to celebrate and feast with them.

'But that was not to be, for who should appear on the battlefield, but Balor's own grandson, Lugh. His doom had finally come to meet him.

'With one lucky shot from his slingshot, Lugh struck Balor in the eye, killing him dead.'

Becca took in a deep breath and Cat noticed she was gripping the seat of her armchair so tight her knuckles had turned white.

'Cethlenn let out a mighty cry seeing her beloved husband struck down before her,' she continued. 'Through her anguish and grief, she bent down and picked up a spear, hurling it toward the Tuatha Dé Danann's forces with all her might. Her aim was true, for it struck the Dagda in his side. The injury wounded him greatly, but it came too late to turn the tides of war. With the death of their great leader, the Formorians could no longer stand against their enemy. The remaining Fomorian forces retreated to safety and the Tuatha Dé Danann were soon declared victors.

'The Dagda and his army arrived at Brú na Bóinne, ready to celebrate their victory, but the festivities were halted when the Dagda discovered the theft of his precious harp. He knew exactly what must have occurred. Although he was exhausted from battle and mortally wounded, he rounded up a small group of loyal companions and headed into the night, determined to steal it back.'

Cat leaned in closer, drawn forward by the passion in Becca's voice. 'What happened?' she asked, her voice almost a whisper.

'They managed to sneak into the Fomorian fortress undetected and located the harp hanging on the wall of the great hall. As soon as the Dagda laid hands on *Uaithne*, the Fomorians let out a mighty roar and prepared to attack. But it was too late. The Dagda began to play the harp, first causing the Fomorians to break out into uncontrolled laughter. They laughed until they ached, until they would have given anything for it to stop. Then he played again, causing the Fomorians to burst into tears and their cries were so heart-rending it set the dogs in the courtyard howling and wailing alongside them. Finally, he played the harp a third time and sent the Fomorians into a deep slumber that lasted many hours. By the time they woke, they found that the Tuatha Dé Danann and the harp were long gone.

'The Dagda died shortly after, succumbing to the wounds he received in battle. No one knew what became of his harp but there were rumours that, before he passed into the Otherworld, the Dagda hid his harp somewhere no one would ever be able to find it again.

'When Cethlenn learned what had transpired, she swore an oath that she would find the harp and use it to get vengeance on her enemies – on the Tuatha Dé Danann and on Lugh, her own grandson, the man who had stolen her beloved Balor from her. She wandered the land in disguise, searching for the harp, chasing down every rumour and hint, until one day, she found out where it was hidden.'

'And did she take the harp?' asked Cat, completely enthralled by the story she was hearing. Granny was a wonderful storyteller, but this was something else. She felt as though the very house itself was holding its breath, waiting to hear what happened next.

Becca sat back and sighed. 'She did not. For it was hidden in a place forbidden to her. The island of Hy-Brasil – a place out of time, protected by the strongest of magics which forbid any Fomorian from setting foot there. It seemed impossible. But Cethlenn was a patient woman. She knew that if she bided her time, she would one day find someone strong and brave enough to retrieve the harp for her. Someone like you.'

Becca suddenly leaned forward and stared into Cat's eyes with such intensity it sent a shiver down her back.

'Think of it, Cat,' said Becca, grabbing Cat by the shoulder with surprising force. 'Think of what you could do if you had such a harp in your hands. Think of the minds you could change. Perhaps, even, your mother's?'

Cat felt her stomach drop. Becca couldn't really be suggesting that the *harp* was the answer to her problems. It was just a legend. Even if it were real, it was wrong to use magic on others like that, wasn't it? As Becca tightened her grip, the discomfort Cat was feeling turned instead to fear. The familiar feeling of dread that had been drowned out by all Becca's talk of witchcraft and magic returned, stronger than ever, and Cat knew she had to get out.

'Thank you for the tea and … and for the story,' she stammered, pulling herself free from Becca. 'But I'm sure Granny will kill me for if I'm late for dinner, so I better go.'

She stood to leave and was met with a sudden flash of power that reached out and curled around her body and held her in place. It was magic, Becca's magic, and she was trapped. She had felt something like this once before, in the fairy fort last Halloween when the Queen of the Fairies used her powers to trap Cat and Shane, and she remembered that bond being impossible to break. She began to panic. Why would Becca do this to her?

Becca stood and Cat's vision seemed to spin. Her vision split and once again there were two figures before her – the Becca she knew and a darker, shadowy presence. It was the shadow she had seen hovering over Becca's shoulder, the one that made her blood turn cold. Cat could see everything clearly now; the shadow had taken over Becca. It had possessed her. When had that happened? And how had she missed it?

'Look into my eyes,' said the thing inside Becca.

'No!' Cat screamed, twisting her head away and screwing her eyes shut. She felt a strong hand grip her by the chin and pull her face back around.

'LOOK AT ME,' the thing inside Becca roared.

Against her will, Cat felt her eyes open, and she realised with horror that Becca's eyes had turned completely white.

'Caitriona Donnelly,' said the thing, infusing Becca's voice with power. 'I place this *geas* on you – when you wake up tomorrow, you will have an overwhelming desire to find the harp of power and you will stop at nothing to get it. You will travel across the waves to Hy-Brasil and seek out its guardian. You will take the harp from her and then return it to me. If you fail to do this, your life will be forfeit. Now leave this place, and do not return until you have found my harp.'

With that, the curse was uttered and the power that had been holding Cat in place faded away.

* * *

Cat blinked, feeling confused and groggy. For a second, she had no idea where she was and was surprised to find that she was still in Becca's house and was being guided out her front door.

'Goodbye Cat,' said Becca. 'It was lovely talking with you today. I look forward to our next meeting.'

'Thanks,' said Cat, shaking her head to try and clear her thoughts. Had she fallen asleep? That was kind of embarrassing. She had been listening to Becca tell a story about an ancient battle and then… then she was standing up, lifting her schoolbag and heading for the door.

Whatever happened, it couldn't have been too bad, Cat thought. *Becca seemed as pleasant as ever when she said goodbye.*

The cold February air hit her cheeks and Cat realised with a start that it was already dark out. She hurried home and hoped that Granny wouldn't be too mad at her.

CHAPTER EIGHT

An Idea is Formed

Cat woke up with an idea. It must have formed in her sleep, she thought, from that story that Becca had told her about that battle between the Tuatha Dé Danann and those other people… the Femur? The Fomo? Cat couldn‹t quite remember and cursed herself once again for not having her Book of Secrets on hand during the story. The one part she *did* remember clearly though, was the bit about the Dagda's harp, *Uaithne.* The harp of power. The one that could change people's feelings. The one that could, just possibly, change her mother's feelings toward Darren.

If I can get my hands on the harp, maybe things can go back to the way they were before.

The thought made her feel a little queasy. She had grown up listening to Granny tell stories about the responsibility that comes with magic use, and she was sure that the older woman would never approve of her idea.

You can't play around with people's feelings, Caitriona! she could almost hear Granny saying. *It isn't right.*

And yet, there was another voice in her head, one that spoke in tones barely above a whisper that told her this was something she needed to do. Something she was *supposed* to do.

Granny had always told Cat to trust her instincts and they would never lead her astray. Surely getting the harp must the right course of action then?

Mam said it herself – she was happy when it was just me, her and Mikey, Cat thought. *Besides, she'll never even know what happened.*

She pushed aside the worry and guilt and began to plan.

She spent all day at school only half-listening to Mr Brennan's lessons. He was teaching them about birds and their migration patterns, which was something Cat would normally find interesting, but all she could think about was how she could go about getting the Dagda's harp. It would be difficult, but hadn't she done difficult things before? She was the girl who had taken on the fairies and won. 'Cat-of-the-Fairies – the girl who sees things others cannot.'

She turned to a blank page in her copybook and began writing out what she already knew.

First things first, the harp was being kept somewhere called 'Hy-Brasil', which a quick Google search that morning before breakfast told her was a mythical island off the west coast of Ireland that was hidden away from most mortal eyes by a veil of mist, although there were reports of people spotting it every seven years or so. She wrote:

Problem One: figure out how to get to Hy-Brasil.

The second thing she knew was that the harp was being protected by some kind of guardian. *That could mean anything*, Cat thought. *It could be a person, or it could be something worse.* She knew from experience that monsters were real and if she wanted something guarded for all eternity that's definitely what she would choose to protect it. There was no way of knowing what she faced until she got there, but still she wrote it down.

Problem Two: figure out how to get the harp away from the guardian.

The third thing she knew was that she needed to give the harp to Becca, but she couldn't remember why...

Did she say she needed it for her research?

When she tried to think too hard about it, Cat felt a faint buzzing between her ears as though she was getting a headache. She decided it didn't matter why Becca needed the harp and added it to her list anyway.

Problem Three: Get the harp off the island and give it to Becca... but only after I use it first.

When the final bell rang, Cat once again brushed her friends off and headed for home. She could see the hurt written all over Ebele's face and felt a small pang of guilt. She hadn't spent any time with her friends this week and she knew that they were probably all wondering if she had fallen out with them. Cat promised herself she'd make it up to them. Once she had the harp and everything was back to normal at home, she would be free to hang out with her friends again.

She was so deep in her own thoughts she didn't realise that Shane had fallen into step beside her.

'Hi,' he said.

'Hi,' Cat replied.

'Look, you're acting weird today and we both know it's something to do with your mam so just spit it out and tell me what's wrong,' said Shane with a directness that surprised Cat.

She thought about lying. Telling him to mind his own business and leave her alone. But then she thought about how much easier it would be to get the harp if she had Shane by her side. After all, he had helped her out of some dangerous situations on Halloween night. If she told him her plan, would he go along with it?

'You're my best friend, Cat,' he said, when she still didn't reply. 'You know you can tell me whatever's wrong.'

That decided it for her.

Cat told him everything. She told him how upset she'd been yesterday when none of her friends offered her any sympathy. She told him about how she bumped into Becca and went back to her house for tea and scones and how Becca listened to her, *really* listened to her. She told him about the tarot cards and how she had opened up to Becca about her Sight. Then she told him the story Becca told her. The one about the Dagda and the harp of power.

'I think she wants me to find it for her,' Cat said. 'I think she needs it in her research or with one of her spells or something ... I don't remember. But she told me where I can find it and I think I have an idea of how I can get there, but...' Cat paused, and looked Shane in the eye. 'But I think I need your help.'

'OK,' said Shane, looking confused. 'I can see why a mythical object would be interesting to a witch and all but, I dunno, Cat. It all sounds a bit—'

'Oh, come on!' Cat said, cutting across him. 'It'll be an adventure! And just think of how happy Becca will be if we can get the harp for her. She might even teach us some witchy things in return. That'd be cool, right?'

Shane scratched his head and Cat knew from experience that was something he only did when he was trying to work through a problem. 'Why can't she just get it herself? If she knows where it is and all...' he asked.

Cat opened her mouth to answer but a sudden static buzzing filled her brain. She knew there was a reason why it had to be her, but whatever it was floated away from her like a balloon that was just out of reach.

'I ... I don't know,' she said lamely. 'But there's another reason why it needs to be us that gets the harp. Shane, this thing can change how people *feel*. Think about it. If we get the harp for Becca I bet she'd let us use it first. I can use it on my mam and make her forget all about Darren. I can make it all like it was before.'

Shane's face fell and Cat knew before he said a word that she had said too much too soon.

'That's a horrible thing to do to someone!' he said. 'You can't just make your mam fall out of love. It isn't fair and I can't believe you'd even think about doing something like that.'

'Shane, I—'

'No. I don't want any part in your plan.'

Cat felt the truth of his words hit her. It *was* unfair. She knew that. She had known it since the first germ of an idea had wiggled into her brain that morning. And yet, she couldn't ignore the small voice in her head telling her it had to be done, that getting the harp was for the greater good.

Instead of agreeing with Shane, she got angry.

'Fine,' she said. 'See if I care. I don't need your help anyway.'

Before he had a chance to say anything else that made her feel worse than she already did, Cat stormed off.

* * *

Shane stood still for a few moments, watching Cat as she walked away from him, hands balled into fists at her side. She had never yelled at him like that before. It was entirely unlike her. Where was his brave, loyal friend? The one who risked everything to save her brother and his sister? She would never even consider doing something so mean-spirited. There had to be something deeply wrong, he thought.

He considered going after her, but decided it would be best if he let her sleep on it. Surely now that she'd said her plan out loud, she would realise how crazy it was and calm down? He truly hoped so.

Once Cat was out of sight, Shane headed for home. Brian mentioned that he was making fajitas for dinner tonight, one of Shane's absolute favourites. Another benefit of having his uncle around so much these days was that Shane was eating very well.

When he opened the door, he found the house was unusually quiet. Normally he would be greeted by the sound of the radio blaring and Brian and Jenny's off-tune singing, but today there was only silence. Confused, he walked into the kitchen and found Brian standing at the breakfast bar, cutting onions for dinner.

'Hey, kiddo,' Brian said, looking up at Shane with a sad smile that set alarm bells ringing in his head. 'How was school today?'

'It was fine… what's going on, Bri? Where's mam and Jenny?'

Brian sighed and put the knife down.

'Jenny's in the living room watching TV,' he said. 'Your mam… well, she's having a bad day. She's gone to bed to lie down, and I don't want to disturb her. Poor thing hasn't been sleeping well.'

She hadn't? This was news to him. His mother had been so happy the past few weeks. So full of life. He thought things were OK, that the bad days were behind them forever.

'But I thought she was better?' said Shane, feeling like his whole world was crashing in on him again. 'She's been doing so well lately, and she's been laughing loads.'

'I know, Shane,' said Brian, putting an arm around his shoulders. The smell of onions was strong on his hands and Shane let himself believe that was the reason why his eyes were starting to fill up with tears. 'And she *is* doing well, overall. But healing takes time. It's not always straightforward. She'll have good days again, but sometimes she'll have bad days too. Those are the days she needs us to be strong for her.'

'Can I go up and see her?' Shane asked, discreetly wiping his eyes on his sleeve.

'Better just let her rest for another while,' Brian said. 'Why don't you go in and keep Jenny company until dinner's ready?'

Shane wandered into the living room in a daze. Jenny was curled up on the couch clutching her ratty old teddy – the one he had won at the carnival with his dad when Jenny was just a baby. She was sucking her thumb, something he and Brian would usually tell her stop doing because they knew it made her skin sore. Today, Shane said nothing. He plonked himself beside her, barely registering the cartoon that was playing.

'Mammy was crying again,' Jenny said as she moved to tuck herself into the crook of Shane's arm. Shane didn't elbow her out of the way or ask her to move like he normally would. He let her sit beside him and allowed the news he had just heard wash over him.

She's having a bad day, he thought. *And there'll be more of them.*

Suddenly, Shane felt completely stupid. The past few weeks had been like a dream, and he had begun to believe that this was it – they were finally out of the dark. Now here they were again, back to being quiet and tiptoeing around the house so they wouldn't upset her.

He remembered the sound of his mother's laugh. He thought about much he had missed it during the bad times and how he wasn't ready to lose it again. Why *couldn't* she just feel good all the time, now? It wasn't fair, she'd had enough hard times.

He came to a decision.

He wriggled free of Jenny and headed into the kitchen.

'Uncle Bri? Can I call over to Cat for a few minutes? I forgot … there's something I need to give her.'

'Sure kiddo, but be back soon. Dinner's almost ready.'

Shane opened the door and hopped over the fence into Cat's front garden. He knocked on the door and when Cat opened it, before she could say a word, he said, 'I'm in. I'll help you get the harp.'

Cat smiled and Shane began to feel a tiny bit better. He would help his mother the only way he could, and everything would be right again.

'How are we going to do it though?' he asked.

'Don't worry,' Cat replied. 'I have a plan.'

CHAPTER NINE

What the Stoat Saw

Vinnie was worried. It had been a full day since the thing that was possessing Becca picked him up and threw him out of the house. It had all happened so fast! One minute he had been happily eating scones and the next, a dark force had taken over his friend. Once the reality of the situation hit him, he tried desperately to find a way to get back into the house, but it was no use. The thing inside Becca ignored his squeaks and scrabbles. He would have to be patient and find a way to slip back in unnoticed.

As night drew in, Vinnie realised he needed to find some shelter. It was cold outside and there were other dangers to worry about – foxes who might be in the mood for a stoat-sized snack and cats looking for a fight. He found a hole beneath an old laurel bush that would have to do. He curled up into a ball and began to shiver. He was cold and hungry and feeling sorry for himself. If only Becca had listened to him when he told her that something strange was going on. Ever since they discovered that blasted well, Vinnie had felt like there was an unknown presence following their every move. Becca had been so sure that everything was fine that he had ignored his instincts and carried on as if nothing was wrong. Now look at him – forced to hide in a hole in the garden while some dangerous force took over his best friend's body.

He knew a little about possession, thanks to the hours he spent watching Becca pore over books on magic and the occult, and from what he could remember, time was of the essence. Once someone's spirit was forced out of their body, they started to lose grip on reality and fade away. His connection with Becca ran deep so he knew she was still hanging on, but he needed to find a way to help Becca, and fast!

When morning broke, Vinnie emerged from the hole.

WHAT THE STOAT SAW

Hiding wasn't doing anyone any good. It was time for him to step up and help his witch in whatever way he could. The first step, he thought, was surveillance.

Mustering all his courage, Vinnie crept up to the house and peered into the kitchen and living room. There was no sign of Becca or the thing that was pretending to her. Next, he scurried up the drainpipe until he reached the upstairs bedroom. He shimmied onto the window ledge and slowly raised his head until he was able to peek in. There she was. The thing pretending to be Becca sat in front of a mirror brushing her hair. She wore a cruel smile on her face that made Vinnie shiver. This was definitely not the woman he knew.

The window was open a crack and Vinnie was just contemplating squeezing through it to better spy on the impostor when all of a sudden she put down the brush and spoke.

'I know you're there,' she said. Vinnie jumped back in surprise, almost falling from the window ledge.

'I can feel your spirit battling hard, little witch,' she continued. 'But it's useless. This body is mine now.'

Vinnie's tiny heart pounded hard in his chest. She

wasn't speaking to him! But that must mean—

He concentrated as hard as he could, and there it was, a faint silvery glow hovering behind the impostor-Becca. It so faint he would never have seen it without his superior stoatly vision, but it was *there*, and it seemed to be fighting. Now *that* was the Becca he knew.

'Time is ticking, little witch,' said the impostor. 'My strength is returning by the minute and soon I'll be strong enough to crush your soul like a ripe blackberry. Better that you leave now while you still can.'

With that, impostor-Becca stood and left the room. The silvery glow that was the real Becca seemed to sag slightly, already defeated. When Vinnie was sure they were alone, he wriggled through the open window.

'Psst, Becca,' he said. 'It's me!'

The silvery shape floated toward him and though he had to strain to hear it, Vinnie could hear her voice calling out to him.

'Vinnie! What are you doing here?'

'I'm here to help you. Just tell me what to do.'

'It's too late, she's too powerful for me. I … I can feel myself slipping away,' as she spoke, her voice did indeed seem to grow fainter and Vinnie began to panic.

'We have to *try*.'

'I ... I'm sorry,' Becca said, with a sob. 'It's so hard to think right now. Everything feels so muddled and confusing...'

'If you had a body, I'd bite your arm so hard right now!' he said. 'There has to be some way to help. I could go and get your mother? She's a powerful witch, surely she can help.'

Becca's spirit shook her head. 'She's in the South of France, remember?'

Vinnie's heart sank. He had forgotten that she had moved there last year after she retired.

'Is there no other option?'

'No, I ... don't think so. But Vinnie, there's ...something else you should know. The thing that possessed me ... she's done something terrible.'

Becca told Vinnie all about Cethlenn and the *geas* she had placed on Cat, her voice slipping in and out as she struggled to hold on to her spirit form.

'A *geas*,' said Vinnie, chewing his lip thoughtfully. 'That's a curse, right?'

'More like … a magical obligation – when you place someone under a *geas* it means they *have* to do what you command them to or … or they'll die.'

'That's not good,' said Vinnie, thinking about the poor young girl being under the Fomorian's control. 'How do we break it?'

Becca shook her silvery head. 'The *geas* can't be broken, that's the point of it … but I think it can be …' The voice of Becca was growing fainter, and Vinnie had to strain to hear her.

'It can be what? Hurry Becca!'

For a long time she was silent and Vinnie worried that maybe she was really gone, but finally she said, 'It can be … manipulated. It's too late for me. Find Cat … help her…'

The silvery haze that was Becca seemed to dim as her voice grew silent and Vinnie felt his fur stand on end.

'Save your energy. I'll find the girl and I'll help her, I promise. And then together we'll help *you*! I'm not giving up on you yet.'

Without turning back, he scurried out the window and shimmied back down the drainpipe. He needed to find

Cat, and soon. Becca was a strong witch, or at least, she had the potential to be, but Vinnie didn't like how much her light had already dimmed.

Hold on, he thought as he tore through the garden into the estate. *Please, hold on.*

CHAPTER TEN

How to Catch a Clurichaun ... Again

When Cat said she had a plan, Shane didn't realise it would involve trudging through a muddy field at eight in the morning while wearing their school uniforms. His shoes were already caked with dirt, and he dreaded to think what Mr Brennan would say when they arrived in the classroom all wet and mucky.

When he said as much to Cat, she replied with a mischievous grin.

'We're not going to school today,'

'What?' Shane stopped dead in his tracks.

'I said we're not going to school. That's the first part of

the plan.'

'Uh-uh, no way! Not doing it. I can't miss school. Brian would kill me if he found out.'

'Don't be such a wuss. We *have* to skip school.' said Cat. 'It gives us the whole day to search for the harp without anyone realising we're gone.'

'Couldn't we go tomorrow instead?' Shane pleaded. 'Tomorrow's Saturday. We can just say we're going over to Karol's or the twins' house or something. No one would think twice about that.'

Cat looked down at her sodden feet, the dampness already spreading up the legs of her school uniform. Maybe Shane was right, maybe it did make more sense to go on a Saturday. After all, it was only one more day and— A sudden pain in her head made her cry out.

'Are you OK?' Shane asked with concern in his voice.

'I'm fine,' Cat said, rubbing her temples. 'It's just a headache. Look, we're already on the way. Let's just go and get it over with, OK? The sooner we have the harp, the sooner we can set everything to rights.'

Cat could tell Shane wanted to argue some more, but luckily for her he just nodded. Immediately, she felt the pain in her head ease. She took a steadying breath and continued across the field.

Ever since she woke up the previous morning with the idea of retrieving the harp of power, it was as though something inside of her was pushing her forward, a little voice that whispered in her ear and told her she needed to hurry. Nothing in her life had ever felt so urgent – not even on Halloween night when she knew she only had until daybreak to get Mikey back from the fairies. She knew it wasn't normal, but she tried to put it out of her mind and concentrate on the task at hand.

'Anyway,' she said, trying to put Shane at ease. 'Don't worry about our parents finding out. If the school calls them to tell them we didn't show up today, we can just use the harp to calm them down. Easy!'

'It doesn't bother you, using the harp like that?' Shane said.

'What do you mean?'

'I don't know, it just doesn't seem right to play with people's minds.'

'We're not *playing* with anyone's minds,' Cat snapped. 'We're going to use the harp to *help* people – you're going to help your mam feel better and I'm going to help mine realise that things were fine before Darren came along.'

Shane rubbed his neck, and his face flushed a deep red. Cat knew he was struggling with something, and she had a horrible feeling she knew exactly what he was going to say.

'I know how it sounds,' she said, trying to convince herself as much as him, 'but ever since my mam told me about her and Darren, I've been miserable and that's made *her* miserable. If her feelings for Darren go away, then we'll *both* be happy again. So if you think about it, it's actually for the greater good. And I promise we won't use the harp any more than we have to, OK? Once we've helped our mams we'll hand it over to Becca and never touch it again.'

Shane nodded, but Cat could still see the doubt written all over his face. She quickened her pace and tried to ignore the part of her that wondered if Shane was right.

'Where are we going anyway?' asked Shane, as he jogged to catch up.

'We're going to my granny's house.' Cat replied.

'We're going *where*? Won't she just send us straight to

school?'

Cat smiled. 'Not if she doesn't see us.'

Normally the walk to Granny's house was relatively straightforward. After leaving the estate, you would turn right, walk up the road a bit and then turn left onto main street. From there it was about a ten-minute walk through the town until you came to the country road that branched off toward Cullane Woods. Granny's house sat just a few metres down that road, but to get there would mean passing the school and risk being spotted. That was the last thing either of them wanted, so they were forced to take the much longer, and much muckier, route through the fields that lay between the estate and Granny's back garden.

Shane kept shooting glances over his shoulder, certain that at any moment the farmer who owned this land would appear and yell at them.

'We're almost there,' Cat said. 'Stop being so twitchy!'

'I'm not twitchy!' Shane protested but he was cut off by Cat's elbow digging him in the ribs.

'Shh!' she said.

Since Granny lived just out of town, her back garden

didn't have a wall or a fence, but was instead separated from the surrounding fields by a thick row of bushes that grew about as tall as Cat's head. As they approached the bushes, she ducked down low and gestured for Shane to do the same. She knew Granny would still be at home this early in the day so they would need to be quiet and careful.

'What do we do now?' Shane whispered.

'Now we catch the Clurichaun.'

Shane raised his eyebrows in surprise. That definitely wasn't what he expected. Cat grinned. The idea had come to her last night when she was lying in bed. She needed to find a way to get to Hy-Brasil and since she couldn't exactly ask anyone to take her there, she was left with only one option. She just needed a way to convince him.

Cat slipped her schoolbag off her shoulder and pulled out a brand-new Jamie Oliver cookbook. Her mother had bought it last year when she went through a phase of wanting to be better in the kitchen. It was a noble goal, but since she could barely manage to boil an egg without causing a fire, the book lay forgotten under old issues of *RSVP* magazine. Cat knew her mother would never miss it. She also knew that with the Clurichaun's new-found love of cuisine, he would be unable to resist taking a peek.

She pulled a ball of twine out of her bag and threaded it through the book, forming a kind of lasso. Then she shoved the book through the bushes, making sure it was face up, and sat back on the grass holding the other length of string tightly.

'Um, what are you doing?' asked Shane, looking at Cat as though she had finally lost her marbles.

'I'm setting a lure for the Clurichaun.'

'And how do you know he'll even see it?'

Cat smiled. 'He will.'

She had chosen their waiting spot carefully. Granny was nothing if not a creature of habit and every Friday morning, as regular as clockwork, she would wash the bed linen. Ever since the Clurichaun had come on the scene, hanging them on the washing line was his job. Looking through a gap in the hedge, Cat could just make out the base of the washing line and the cookbook lying perfectly in front of it.

'Now we wait,' she said.

It turned out they didn't have long to wait. After a few

minutes, they heard the back door creak open and the sound of a male voice singing off-tune. 'Oh me, oh my, you make me sigh...'

Cat peeked between the bushes and saw the Clurichaun struggling down the path toward the washing line hauling a laundry basket that was almost as big as he was.

'... when people stop and people stare you know it fills my heart with— oh, hello. What do we have here?' The singing stopped. He must have spotted the book.

Cat looked at Shane and mouthed the words 'Get ready.'

She listened to the crunch of gravel as the Clurichaun came closer and, just as he reached out to grab the book, Cat tugged the string and pulled the book closer.

'Hmm,' said the Clurichaun. 'That's ... odd.'

He took a step closer, reaching again for the book and once again Cat pulled it closer to her.

'What the—?'

He took another step and was now just on the other side of the bush.

'Now!' Cat whispered and together, she and Shane reached through the bush and grabbed the Clurichaun, pulling him through to the other side. He let out a panicked yelp, that quickly turned into a sigh when he saw who his attackers were.

'Hello,' said Cat brightly. 'We need your help.'

'Not you two again,' said the Clurichaun with a groan. 'No nasty salt circle this time?'

He was referring to Halloween night, when Cat had lured him into a trap and forced him to give her information about the fairies so she could save her brother.

She shook her head. 'No trap this time. Just a deal.'

The Clurichaun raised a wiry grey eyebrow. 'Oh? And why would I help you after you sneaking up on me like that?'

'Technically, you were the one who came to us,' said Shane. 'And really, when the book started moving, did you not wonder what was going on?'

'Ah yeah, 'twas a bit odd all right…'

'We just want to talk to you for a second,' said Cat. 'Please, hear us out and then decide.'

The Clurichaun eyed the cookbook that Cat was now holding.

'Is that the fifteen-minute meals one?' he asked.

Cat nodded.

'I haven't read that one… All right, tell me what it is ye're up to and *maybe* I'll consider helping you.'

Cat took a breath, she needed to play this right. If the Clurichaun declined or if he called out for Granny, then the plan was over before it had even begun.

'We were thinking that things must be awful boring for you lately. You spend all your time cooking and cleaning for Granny.'

The Clurichaun shrugged, 'Ah, 'tis no bother really …'

'But you must miss your old life, just a little bit?' Cat asked. 'After all, it's been ages since you've gotten to do something fun.'

'I have fun,' said the Clurichaun. 'Just last night I was tellin' your Granny all about this new knife sharpener I stole – uh, I mean, this new knife sharpener I *found* in Kitchen Stuff Plus and—

'Oh come on!' said Cat, cutting across him. 'You're a *fairy*! Mischief is in your blood. Where has your sense of adventure gone?'

The Clurichaun's nostrils flared in annoyance and Cat could see she almost had him.

'That's actually why we came here today. Me and Shane are planning a little adventure of our own and we thought you could help to get things started, but if you're too much of a chicken…'

The Clurichaun eyed her suspiciously.

'What kind of adventure?' he said.

'Oh, nothing dangerous, I swear!' Cat felt the lie slip off her tongue. Fairies couldn't lie themselves and she hoped that meant they weren't good at detecting lies in others. 'We'll even be back by dinner.'

She waved the cookbook at him. 'If you help us out, I'll get you more of these,' she said. 'Maybe even the Italian one…'

Finally, he caved. He snatched the book out of her hands and began flipping through it.

'Fine. We have a deal. Now tell me what you need me to do.'

'Not so fast,' said Cat. 'I need you to *promise* that you'll take us where we need to go and that you won't say a word to my granny.'

She stuck out her hand and as the Clurichaun grasped it in his own, Cat felt a small surge of magic pass between them that meant the bond was sealed.

'I promise, now tell me what you need me to do.'

'We need you to take us to Hy-Brasil.'

The Clurichaun's face dropped. 'Hy-Brasil ... what would you be doing there?'

'Don't worry about that,' said Cat. 'You only need to worry about getting us there.'

'No way, not going to happen,' said the Clurichaun firmly. 'I couldn't take you there, even if I wanted to – which I *don't*!'

'Why not?'

'The island is warded. No one can use magic to enter, save the Tuatha Dé Danann themselves. If I tried to use my magic to take us there, it'd fling us off somewhere in the middle of the Atlantic Ocean.'

'Well,' said Cat, chewing her lip. 'What if you got us close? Just bring us as close to the wards as you possibly can and then we can make our own way.'

The Clurichaun tugged at his scraggly grey beard. 'You don't understand. There are dangers there, girl. Even now, there are stories of beasts that walk as men and a powerful ancient evil that guards the island from intruders.'

Shane had gone pale. 'Cat, maybe this isn't—'

She couldn't let him finish that sentence. 'You made a promise,' she said to the Clurichaun. 'It's too late to back out now.'

'What if we did something else?' the Clurichaun pleaded. 'I could take ye to see one of the legendary fairy hurling matches sometime? That would be a fun adventure, wouldn't it? Or how about finding the Salmon of Knowledge?'

'Didn't Fionn mac Cumhaill eat that like, thousands of years ago?' asked Shane.

'Yes, but there's probably another one knocking around by now,' said the Clurichaun. 'Come on. Surely that'd be more fun for ye?'

He looked at Cat with such hopefulness that it broke her heart a little. She shook her head. 'It has to be Hy-Brasil.'

She could see the battle play out on the Clurichaun's face, but he knew as well as she did that it was no good. Fairy bargains couldn't be broken.

Finally, he sighed in defeat. 'I don't like this, girl, and I don't like that you tricked me.'

'I'm sorry,' said Cat. 'But we had to.'

With a grumble he grabbed both Cat and Shane by the arm and said, 'Hold on, this won't be a fun ride.'

Suddenly, the world dropped away.

CHAPTER ELEVEN

Sailing for Hy-Brasil

Cat felt as though she had just stepped off a roller coaster. One moment she was in a mucky field out the back of her Granny's house and then in the blink of an eye, she was standing on a rocky shoreline, looking out over the sea. She tried to steady herself, but it was no use. Her legs gave way and she fell to the ground, hard enough to make her yelp in pain. She would probably have a bruise, but at least she was faring better than Shane. He stumbled off to retch into a rock pool.

'Good lad,' said the Clurichaun, patting him on the back. 'Get it all up. Better out than in, that's what I always say!'

'What just happened?' asked Shane, wiping his mouth.

'Ye travelled by the fairy road. It's fast but it does take some getting used to, especially for humans.'

When Cat felt like she could stand again, she hauled herself to her feet and took in her surroundings. They were on a narrow pebble beach with small cliffs flanking each side, forming a natural harbour. It was a clear, calm spring day. Even the Atlantic Ocean was far from its usual wild self. The water was so still it almost looked like a mirror reflecting the sky above and when Cat looked out over the horizon it seemed as though she could see for miles and miles.

'Is this it?' she asked, her voice slow and heavy, as though she had only woken up. 'Did you manage to get us to Hy-Brasil?'

The Clurichaun shook his head. 'No, I told you, girl. The island is warded from the likes of me. This is as close as I can bring you.'

'So we're still on the mainland?'

'You are. But look,' he pointed a gnarled finger out over the water. 'Way out over that direction, can you see it?'

Cat squinted out over the water but there was nothing

there.

'No, I can't see anything.'

'Look again, girl. This time use your Sight.'

Cat nodded. Of course. Hy-Brasil was a magical island so it made sense that she wouldn't be able to just *see* it. She would need to tap into her power. Cat used to believe the Sight was something completely out of her control. She thought it was just something that *happened* to her, not a tool that she could use to her advantage. But when she and Shane were lost on Halloween night and couldn't find their way to the fairy fort known as the Green Rath, Shane had encouraged her to try using the Sight to guide them right to the fairy's front door. And it had worked! Cat had been able to feel the magic tugging on her senses, showing her the way. That first time, it had been difficult to tap into the Sight, but after months of practice, it had almost become easy.

She took a deep breath, closed her eyes and began to concentrate. At first, there was nothing unusual, only the sound of water gently lapping against stone and the cry of a seagull somewhere overhead. But as she took another deep breath and allowed her mind to open up, she felt it, the familiar pull of magic. She opened her eyes and there, in the distance, was a hazy outline of an island.

'I can see it!' she said.

'Are you sure?' asked Shane, squinting out over the water. 'I can't see anything.'

'The Clurichaun was right, you need the Sight to see it. But… something about it looks strange. Like it's all foggy or something.'

'Aye, well that'd be the protective wards I told ye about,' said the Clurichaun. 'It's said that the island is shrouded in a thick layer of mist to protect it from intruders.'

Cat bit her lip. The island looked so far away. How were they ever going to get there?

As if reading her mind, the Clurichaun gave an exaggerated stretch and said, 'Well, I suppose I'll be off now…'

She whipped round to face him. 'What? No, you can't go yet.'

'Why not? I've done my part. I've taken ye as far as I can. No sense in me hanging around. Once you realise it's a fool's errand you're on, give me a call and maybe I'll help ye out.'

Cat began to panic. He couldn't leave them here, there

had to be another way to get them to the island. Just then, her eyes landed on something.

'Wait!' she yelled. 'You made a promise to take us as close to the wards as you possibly can.'

'Yes,' replied the Clurichaun, 'and as I explained, this is as close as I'm able to bring you.'

Cat grinned and there was a wicked gleam in her eye. She reached out a hand and pointed to a small wooden rowing boat propped up on the rocks.

'I think that will help us get a little closer.'

The Clurichaun's shoulders slumped in defeat. 'Sometimes, you're too smart for your own good girl.'

'Um, Cat,' said Shane, hurrying to catch up with Cat as she strode across the beach toward the boat. 'Do you even know how to row a boat? One that size... it'll be hard work.'

'I know,' replied Cat. 'But we won't need to row it too far. The Clurichaun's magic will propel us most of the way. We'll just need to make it through the wards and onto the shore.'

'And you're sure we can do that?' asked Shane. 'Aren't wards meant to, you know, keep people away?'

'The Clurichaun said that no *magic* could be used to get through the wards. He didn't say anything about sailing through it in a boat. I'm sure we'll be fine.'

When they reached the boat, Cat felt her confidence in the plan shatter. It had clearly been abandoned for quite some time and although she couldn't make out any obvious holes, it didn't seem like the sturdiest vessel to ever travel the seas. She just hoped it would hold together long enough to get them to the island and back. The 'and back' part was also troubling her – the Clurichaun only agreed to help them on their way there. Once they were on the island, they would be on their own. That something she'd have to deal with later. Right now, the first problem they needed to solve was how to get the boat into the water.

She and Shane tried pushing it upright, but it was heavier than it looked.

'What is this thing made of? Lead?' said Shane.

'You could help, you know,' said Cat to the Clurichaun, who was looking on amusement.

'I *could*, but I'm having a grand old time right where I am.'

'The sooner we get to the island, the sooner we can get

home again … it would be an awful shame if we were delayed so long that Granny found out we were missing, wouldn't it?'

'Bah!' said the Clurichaun, throwing his hands in the air. 'Out of the way, so.'

Cat and Shane stepped back and watched as the boat rose up slightly in the air, clearing the pebbles of the beach by only a few centimetres, and drifted down toward the water. The Clurichaun let out a loud huff of exhaustion and wiped his brow. 'Phew, haven't done anything like that in a while. I'm a bit out of practice.'

'Thank you,' said Cat.

'I'm not sure you should be thanking me, girl,' he said. 'Now come on, let's go and get this over with.'

They waded out into the water and Shane held the boat steady as first Cat and then the Clurichaun hauled themselves in. Once Shane took a seat, the Clurichaun told them both to hold on tight and suddenly the boat jerked to life.

It was as though they were in a speedboat rather than an old wooden fishing boat and Cat let out a whoop of joy as they cut through the waves like a hot knife through butter. Shane was grinning from ear to ear. He used to go sailing with his dad, she remembered. She twisted in her seat, being careful to keep a tight grip of the hull to avoid being flung into the sea. At the rate they were going, they'd have the harp and be home by lunchtime. Cat smiled. This was all going exactly according to plan.

They had been travelling for fifteen minutes or so when the Clurichaun drew the boat to a halt. The wall of mist was close now. It stretched out before them like a lace curtain, mostly obscuring the island from their view.

'Cat are you seeing this?' said Shane. 'It's mad looking! It's still bright and sunny here but right ahead, it's like a line of fog!'

'This is as far as I can go,' said the Clurichaun. He pointed toward the mist. 'That is the boundary of Hy-Brasil. From here you're on your own.'

Cat bent down and picked up the oars. 'Thank you for getting us here,' she said, really meaning it. 'I'm sorry I tricked you into doing it. I know that wasn't nice of me, but I promise we had a good reason to.'

'Are you sure you need to do this, girl?' said the Clurichaun, and Cat noticed there was genuine fear in his eyes. 'Say the word and I'll take ye home right now and we'll never speak of it again.'

'I'm sure,' she said.

The Clurichaun sighed deeply. 'I don't like that ye tricked me, and I don't think this adventure of yours is a good idea, but after what happened at Halloween, I made a promise to your Granny I'd look out for you. So…' he pulled off his signature red cap and handed it to Cat. His bald head shone in the morning sun. 'Take this and if ye run into trouble – which you probably will – just call out and this will bring you home.'

Cat suddenly felt like crying. Why was he being so kind to her after what she'd just done? Cat resolved to buy him whatever cookbook he wanted (and that her pocket money could afford) to make it up to him.

'Be careful,' said the Clurichaun as he stared into the mist. 'The Tuatha Dé Danann may be gone, but that doesn't mean the island is empty. There are dangers afoot and the island itself doesn't deal with intruders well. Keep your wits about ye and whatever ye came here to do, do it quick.'

With that, he was gone.

'What now?' asked Shane.

'Now, we row.'

Not far now, she told herself, as the boat entered the mist.

She expected it to feel cold and damp against her skin, like the feeling you get when you're sprayed by a hose in the summer, but the mist didn't feel like that. Instead it felt thick and oppressive as though the island didn't want them there. Suddenly, she felt the bow of the boat begin to turn. She began to row harder, trying her best to correct their course.

'What's happening?' cried Shane. 'Why are we spinning.'

'I think you were right,' Cat gasped. 'I think it's the wards trying to keep us out.'

'What do we do?'

'We keep rowing!'

Shane slipped in beside Cat and grabbed an oar. Working together they managed to keep the boat straight, although it felt as though they were battling against giant waves.

'Do you see anything yet?' Shane said.

Cat twisted around but the wall of mist was much thicker than she thought it would be. She couldn't see much further than the bow. 'No, nothing.'

She was beginning to wonder whether the wards had managed to turn them around after all when, all of a sudden, the haze lifted and the island of Hy-Brasil lay ahead of them, perfectly clear in the morning sunshine. Cat gasped at the sight of the tall, imposing cliffs that made up most of the island's rugged coastline. From what she could tell, the landscape seemed empty – it looked to be mostly rocks and grass with little trees – but when she squinted, she could see there was some kind of structure sitting atop the cliff.

That's where the harp will be, she thought. *That's where we need to go.*

'We did it!' she said, grinning at Shane.

'Woah!'

'I know, it's pretty amazing, right?'

'No, it's not that. Um, Cat … tell me you can see somewhere for us to dock?'

Cat scanned the shoreline. There looked to be several narrow inlets ahead. She was sure at least one of them would be a good place for them to disembark and she told Shane as much.

'OK good, because we're taking in water, fast!'

Cat looked down. She had been so entranced by seeing Hy-Brasil, she hadn't noticed the water that was now lapping around her ankles.

'What do we do?' she asked, trying not to panic.

'I … I don't know,' said Shane. 'You try and find the leak while I keep rowing.'

Cat dropped to her knees and felt around the hull, looking for the source of the leak, but it was no use. It seemed to be coming from everywhere and nowhere.

'I can't find it!' Cat yelled.

The water level was higher now, and Shane was struggling with the oars.

'It's too heavy,' he said. 'I can't keep going. How far are we from shore?'

It was hard to tell. It didn't seem to be too far away but at the rate the boat was taking on water, Cat didn't think it would make it.

'I think we need to swim.'

'But … but we've got our schoolbags and coats and…'

'Abandon them!' she yelled, already slipping her backpack off her back. 'Come on, hurry!'

Cat was a good swimmer, but she had only ever swum laps in the pool at the local leisure centre. She had never done any real open-water swimming before. So many worries flashed though her mind – how deep was the water? What if there was a rip tide? Were there sharks in this part of the ocean? She could feel the terror rising in her chest, but she knew if she gave into it that would be the end, so she pushed down her fear and began to swim.

Her arms and lungs were burning and for a while, it seemed as though the shoreline was getting no closer. How was that possible? But finally, Cat felt her fingers brush against sand and she knew it was shallow enough to stand. She pulled herself upright and found that Shane was right behind her. Together they trudged through the shallows toward the beach that lay ahead. Cat almost sobbed with relief as they set foot on dry land.

They collapsed into the sand and spent a few minutes lying on their backs taking deep, calming breaths.

'Please tell me you still have the Clurichaun's cap?' asked Shane.

Cat shoved her hand into the pocket of her uniform trousers, pulled out the sodden red cap and waved it at him.

'Good,' he replied. 'With the boat gone, he's our only way off this island.'

When Cat's heartbeat returned to normal, she pulled herself up onto her feet and tried to ignore how wet and sandy she felt.

'Come on,' she said. 'Let's go get the harp.'

CHAPTER TWELVE

The Watchers

The sun was high in the sky as Cat and Shane made their way off the beach. Cat hoped their uniforms would dry off soon. Her school jumper was sodden with seawater and she could feel her socks squelching in her shoes with every step she took. After struggling over some sand dunes, they paused to take stock of their surroundings. It seemed Cat's first impression of the island had been correct – they found themselves standing on scrubby grassland that sloped upward in a series of rolling hills. There didn't seem to by any proper woodland on this part of the island, but random trees dotted the landscape here and there, their trunks bent sideways by the force of the wind that whipped in over the Atlantic. There were plenty of gorse bushes and their coconutty scent filled the air and reminded Cat of holidays by the sea.

'Where to now?' asked Shane. 'What are your spidey senses telling you?'

Cat didn't even need to concentrate to tap into her Sight here. The pull of magic was so strong she could almost see it spooling out before her like a thread. It was leading upward.

She pointed to the highest peak on the island where a squat stone fortress could be seen.

'That way.'

'Oh, great! I love blindly wandering into a spooky looking fort. That went so well for us last time!'

Cat rolled her eyes at him. 'Oh stop moaning, we got out of the fairy fort in one piece … more or less. Now come on. It's a long way to the top of that hill.'

For the first half an hour or so, their journey was largely uneventful. The flat grassland soon gave way to rocky terrain and Cat found herself wishing she hadn't cast her backpack into the sea. She longed for a sip of water to quench her thirst.

'Hey, have you noticed it's super quiet?' said Shane.

'Yeah, I mean, it's an abandoned island so it's going to be pretty quiet.'

'It's not just that …it's like there's no sign of life at all – no birds singing, no insects buzzing around.'

Cat realised he was right. It was almost like the whole island was muffled by a giant blanket. The effect was eerie.

'We might be the only things on this island making noise,' said Shane.

'Which means we're like a giant beacon right now,' added Cat.

The Clurichaun's warning rang out in her mind: *There are stories of beasts that walk as men.* She had to hope those beasts were the kind that only came out at night.

Shane nodded. 'What do we do?'

'You heard the Clurichaun, we keep our wits about us.'

Now that Shane had pointed it out, Cat couldn't help but notice how loud they were being. Every step they took seemed to echo across the land. Even their breath seemed unbearably loud. How could they possibly make it all the way up to the fortress undetected? Perhaps it was just paranoia, but she began to feel as though there was somebody watching them.

'Cat,' Shane whispered, 'I have a bad feeling.'

'Me too,' she replied. 'It feels like—'

She never got a chance to finish her sentence because just then, they heard a very audible crunch on the trail ahead of them as though someone, or something, had stood on a fallen twig.

'Did you hear that?' Shane hissed.

Cat wanted to reassure him, to reassure *herself*, that it was just a woodland creature going about its business – a fox or even a deer. Her hopes were dashed when a creature stepped out onto the path in front of them and let out a blood-curdling howl. Cat felt her blood freeze as she found herself face to face with an enormous grey wolf.

It was easily twice her size, with a thick, glossy coat of fur and sharp, gleaming teeth. Its eyes were fixed on them.

Cat grabbed Shane's arm so hard it hurt.

'What do we do?' Shane whispered, his voice laced with panic.

'I don't know,' Cat replied. Her mind began to race. Surely this was impossible. Wolves went extinct in Ireland ages ago ... but this wasn't Ireland. This was Hy-Brasil. *A place out of time.*

She took a step backward, pulling Shane with her, her eyes never leaving the creature. The wolf growled low in its throat, a warning. Suddenly, two more wolves appeared to their right and three more to their left.

Panic finally took over.

'Run!' Cat yelled, but as she turned to flee, she discovered they were completely surrounded.

'Halt!' came a deep voice. Cat spun around. The large grey wolf was gone and, in its place, stood a man. He was tall with long, sandy-coloured hair dusted with grey at the temples and he wore an old brown tunic and a forest-green cloak with designs around the edges picked out in gold thread. He had power, Cat could tell that right away, but it felt different to the kind of magic she was used to. This felt raw and wild.

'Who are you, to trespass on this sacred isle?' his voice was a deep, low rumble that sounded almost like a snarl.

Cat opened her mouth to speak, but found that her throat was completely dry. What do you say to a predator?

'Please don't hurt us!' Shane blurted out. 'We don't mean any harm!'

The stranger looked them over with amber eyes, and his expression turned from anger to surprise. 'Children! But this cannot be. How did mere children make it past the wards?'

Shane launched into an explanation and Cat gave him a sharp elbow in the ribs. 'Shut up,' she hissed. They had no idea who these people, these *creatures* were. She didn't want Shane to lay all their cards on the table right now. What if he said something that caused the wolves to attack? Cat needed time to think.

The stranger stroked his moustache and Cat thought he seemed tired. He turned to the two smaller wolves to his left and said, 'Domhnall, Sorcha, take these children to the village. I will deal with them later.' Without another word, he turned his back and walked away.

Two wolves stepped forward and, in a heartbeat, they had shifted into humans. The change was so seamless it made Cat's head spin. They were younger than their leader, only around twenty years old or so, Cat thought. The man called Domhnall was tall and broad with dark, tangled hair and his muscled arms were criss-crossed with old scars. The woman, Sorcha, was short and lean and her bright red hair was braided back from her face revealing a long, jagged scar ran that from her eyebrow to her cheek. These were a dangerous people, Cat thought. A tribe of warriors who were no strangers to a fight. They would have to be careful in all that they said and did.

Sorcha scowled at them but didn't say a word as she grabbed Cat by the arm and dragged her away from the rest of the wolf pack.

'Where are you taking us?' Cat asked.

'Save it, girl,' said Sorcha with a low growl. 'We'll let Conn decide what to do with you.'

'Don't mind her,' said Domhnall, who, despite his size, steered Shane off the trail with a lot less force than Sorcha applied to Cat. 'She isn't used to being around strangers – none of us are – but you may rest assured that her bark is worse than her bite.'

At that, Sorcha snarled but Domhnall just laughed.

The wolf warriors marched Cat and Shane back down hill, cutting away from the trail they had been following. Cat could feel the magic of the harp calling to her and the pain began to rise in her head once again.

You're going the wrong way, a small voice seemed to

whisper in her mind, *Escape your captors and get to the fortress. Hurry!*

How? Cat whispered back. She could feel Sorcha's iron grip clamped around her arm and she knew without a doubt that there was no way she was getting away from her anytime soon.

After a few minutes, they crested a ridge and found themselves staring down at a handful of wooden buildings clustered together in small valley.

The village was surrounded by a high wooden fence and a deep ditch that would make it difficult for enemies to attack. Smoke rose from the thatched roofs of the huts and Cat could hear the bleating of sheep and the barking of dogs.

'You keep *animals* here?' asked Shane, in surprise. 'Won't you ... you know, attack them?'

Sorcha snarled in annoyance, but Domhnall simply laughed. 'No lad, we don't attack the animals. When we're in our wolf forms we do retain some sense of control. These animals are our livelihood, and we take care of them as such.'

'Oh, sorry,' Shane said, blushing slightly.

'Move it,' said Sorcha, shoving Cat down the hill toward the village.

Her eyes were wide as they passed through the gate. She found herself standing in a broad courtyard that was buzzing with activity. There was a young woman tending to some pigs and a blacksmith forging what looked to Cat to be a large sword. Beside him were a group of youths assembling arrows and she noticed that the pile of finished arrows seemed alarmingly large. There were even children here – and Cat saw a group of youths chasing each other around the wooden huts. The contrast between the village and the rest of the island was startling. There was so much *life* here.

'Can *all* of these people turn into wolves?' Cat asked.

'Yes,' said Sorcha. 'So you better watch yourselves.'

They attracted plenty of curious glances as they walked through the courtyard, but a glare from Sorcha made everyone return to their work without saying a word.

Up close, Cat could see the buildings were like nothing she had ever seen before. They were all circular and made out of wood and woven reeds. They had tall, pointed roofs made of straw and their shape reminded her of a circus tent. They had no doors or windows that she could see, but all of them seemed to have narrow openings that would allow people to move in and out.

When they reached the largest of the huts, Sorcha shoved Cat toward the entrance with more force than was necessary.

'Stay inside and wait for Conn,' she said before transforming back into her wolf form and stalking away.

'Are we your prisoners?' Shane blurted out.

Domhnall rubbed his neck and looked awkward. 'No, nothing like that. But we don't get trespassers often so Conn will want to have a word with ye.'

'Is he your leader?' asked Cat.

Domhnall nodded. 'He's the chieftain of our clan. He's a smart man and a fair one at that, but he's also protective of his people. When Conn comes by just be sure to answer his questions truthfully and everything will be grand.'

'What do we do in the meantime?' asked Shane.

'You wait,' said Domhnall. 'Don't worry, I'll be back shortly.' With that, he turned back into a wolf and trotted away.

Despite his assurances that they weren't really prisoners, Cat couldn't help but feel like their every move was being watched. One thing was for sure, they wouldn't be going anywhere soon.

Chapter Thirteen

Among the Wolves

There were no windows inside the hut, so it took Cat's eyes a few moments to adjust to the gloom. They appeared to be standing in one large, round room. Like the outside, the inside walls were also made of wood, but here and there Cat noticed dried animal hides pinned to the walls, perhaps to keep out the cold and damp. The high, circular roof was propped up by a handful of wooden pillars as tall as trees. The floor was strewn with fresh, clean straw and in the centre of the room was a fire pit over which hung a large cooking pot.

'OK, let's go before one of them gets back,' said Shane.

'Sorry, what?' said Cat, confused. Did he not see the

village fortifications and how many members of the wolf-clan were out there?

'The cap!' he said, 'Let's use it to call the Clurichaun and get out of here before Domhnall or that Conn guy get here. Come on, Cat!'

Cat put her hand in her pocket and rubbed the red felt between her fingers. Shane was right; she could call for the Clurichaun right now and they would be home before any of the wolves even knew they were missing. They could forget all about this day and—

Blinding pain flashed through Cat's skull, and she let out a yelp.

'What's happening to you, Cat?'

She could hear the panic in Shane's voice, and she wanted to tell him she didn't know what was wrong with her, but the pain was so bad it was all she could do to keep from falling to the floor.

'You've been getting these headaches all day ... This isn't normal. We need to go right now and get you to a doctor or something.'

'I ... can't,' Cat blurted out. 'I can't leave without ... the harp.'

Shane threw his hands in the air in frustration. 'Who *cares* about the harp? We've been captured by a bunch of werewolves, you're clearly not well and—'

'They're not werewolves,' Cat said, her breathing slowly returning to normal as the pain in her head began to die down.

'Well, what are they then?'

'I … I don't know. I think they're something else.'

'Oh, whatever! Same difference. In case you haven't noticed, they were making weapons out there. Something is going on and I don't think we want to stick around to find out what, so let's *go*.'

Cat shook her head. 'No. I'm sorry, Shane, but I'm not going.' She held out the cap to him. 'Here, you take it. You can call the Clurichaun and go home. I won't blame you or anything but… but I need to see this through to the end.'

'Oh no, if you think I'm leaving you on your own among a pack of heavily armed werewolves—'

'They're not werewolves.'

'WHATEVER!'

Shane stalked to the other side of the room and kicked

over a wooden bucket in frustration. Cat left him to it and settled herself down on the straw-covered floor to try and figure out what their next move would be. The headache wasn't gone, not entirely. But it had moved to a background hum, taking up space beside the little voice that still whispered to her to hurry, to get the harp before it was too late.

Her brooding was interrupted by the sound of Shane rummaging through the hut – searching through clay pots and poking under the straw bedding.

'What are you doing?' she asked.

'Looking for weapons or something we can use to defend ourselves if need be.'

'I don't think they'll hurt us. They could have done that by now if they wanted to. I think they just want to talk.'

'We don't know that for sure yet,' he said. 'I'd rather be safe than sorry.'

Shane had a point, she realised. It would be stupid of them not to at least *try* to find a way to defend themselves. She jumped up and joined him in his search.

'I wonder what's under here…' he said, stooping down to examine a roughly-spun woollen blanket. He pulled it back and let out a yell that made Cat jump.

'What is it?' she asked, as Shane stumbled back toward her.

'Wolf!' he said.

Sure enough, there was indeed a wolf curled up on the floor with its legs and tail tucked in tight to its body. It seemed to be somewhat smaller in size than the wolves they had encountered outside, with a slender frame and fur that was dappled cream and brown. Cat and Shane backed away until they were on the far side of the hut.

'Why isn't it moving?' whispered Cat. 'Is it sleeping?'

'No ... I think she's injured,' Shane replied.

'How can you tell?' said Cat, 'And wait ... how do you know it's a *she*?'

'I don't know...' Shane replied slowly. He had a slightly glazed look, as though he were concentrating on something. 'It's weird, but it's almost like I can hear her.'

'What do you mean you can hear her?' Cat looked at Shane with wide eyes. 'Can you read minds now?'

Shane shook his head. 'No, it's not like that. It's hard to describe but ... listen, can't you hear her whimpering?'

Cat shook her head; she didn't hear anything but the

animal's soft breathing.

'Well, I can hear her and she's trying to tell me something. Maybe if I—'

He took a step toward the wolf, but just then, a shadow appeared at the opening.

'I wouldn't go too close, lad.' It was Domhnall, back in his human form. He was carrying a basket, which he placed down near the fire.

'Why? Is she dangerous?' asked Cat.

Domhnall walked over to the sleeping wolf and picked up the blanket, gently covering her again. 'She isn't well, and she may lash out on instinct if you get too close. Best to just leave her alone.'

Domhnall must have caught the look Cat and Shane exchanged because he quickly added, 'She's not dangerous! But she is not herself right now.'

'What's wrong with her?' Shane asked, looking at the wolf thoughtfully.

'She's sick,' said Domhnall. 'She was injured, oh, a long time ago now. Our healer Ferdia did his best to help her but for some reason she has never fully recovered.'

'How was she injured?' asked Shane at the same time

Cat asked, 'Who *are* you people and what are you going to do with us?'

'So many questions!' said Domhnall, shaking his head.

'Please,' added Cat. 'We honestly didn't have any idea what we were getting into when we came here today. We just what to know what we're dealing with.'

Domhnall looked between them and seemed to soften. 'Well… all right. But first, I have bread and water for you.'

'We're not hungry,' said Cat quickly.

'Speak for yourself,' said Shane.

Cat shot him an angry glare. 'We don't take food from magical creatures, remember?' she whispered to him, but Domhnall's hearing was clearly as good in human form as it was in wolf form because he said, 'It's nothing bad, I promise. It's an old tradition. If you share our food, that makes you our guests and we don't – we *can't* – hurt guests.'

'Maybe we should take some?' whispered Shane. 'To be safe?'

'I don't know…' said Cat, trying to think what Granny would advise in this situation.

'Domhnall seems nice,' said Shane. 'I think he's telling

the truth.'

Cat was still wary, but before she could protest Shane grabbed the bread and shoved a hunk of it into his mouth. When he didn't immediately start choking, Cat deemed it safe enough to take a small bite herself. It was good – warm and fresh.

Domhnall smiled and gestured for them to take a seat.

'Where do I even start?' he said.

'Tell us who you are and how you can turn into wolves,' Cat suggested.

'It's a long story,' said Domhnall.

'We have time,' replied Cat. 'Unless you want to just let us go right now…'

Domhnall laughed and Cat wondered if anything could ruffle his feathers… or his fur, for that matter.

'I'll begin at the beginning. My people have not always had the ability to turn into wolves. For many hundreds of years, we were a normal clan who lived far away from this island in a kingdom that no longer exists, called Ossory. We were a peaceful people, for the most part, living in harmony with the land and trading with the other clans who surrounded us. But time has a way of changing things. There were difficult years when the winter was especially cruel, causing crops to fail and livestock to die. During such desperate times, people grow bold and soon our neighbours became our enemies. They began to encroach on our land and threaten our way of life. We knew we had to do something.

'The druids of our clan told our leader Conn about a powerful sorceress who lived in a cave on the edge of our territory. She was feared and respected by all who knew her, for her magic was said to be stronger than any other in the land. Conn vowed that he would not approach her until all hope was lost. But as the attacks on our home grew more frequent, he knew he could not wait any longer. He made the half-day journey through the forest to the home of the sorceress and asked for her help in defeating our enemies. The sorceress agreed to help us, but warned Conn that her help would come with a price – we would need to give up half of our humanity.

'Conn did not understand, and the sorceress refused to explain, but our people were desperate and so Conn agreed. Once the deal was struck, the sorceress cast a powerful spell that would give us the strength and ferocity of wolves. We would be able to defeat our enemies and protect our land. So thrilled were we with this newfound power that it took many years for us to realise what a terrible cost we had paid and what losing half our humanity really meant. The sorceress had cursed us to live forever as half-human, half animal, shunned by those we once considered friends and forced into hiding. So we remain to this day.'

'But you're human right now,' said Cat. 'You seem to be well able to control it. Why did you need to hide?'

'We can control our powers to an extent,' said Domhnall. 'But it took many hundreds of years to get to this point. Even so, living as we do means that we are always under some kind of threat. We have learned to be vigilant.'

'You've been cursed for *hundreds* of years?!' Cat said. *No wonder Sorcha is so nasty,* she thought. *She isn't used to being around strangers!*

'Can I ask… what happened to her?' said Shane, who was still watching the injured she-wolf closely.

Domhnall sighted. '*That* is a sad story indeed. In the years after the curse was placed upon us, word of our ferocity in battle began to spread. Most people kept well away from the plains of Ossory, but there are plenty of people who fear what they do not understand and will seek to dominate it. We were subject to many attacks, mostly from young men and women seeking to prove themselves as heroes or from self-proclaimed "monster hunters" who sought to rid the land of our kind.

'One day, many years ago now, a small group of us were patrolling the eastern edge of our border. We were led by Una, Conn's wife and second only to him in ruling the tribe. When we were set upon by a band of warriors, she took it on herself to protect us, the youngest members of the tribe, from harm. She attacked the bandits in her wolf form, but did not realise that they were armed with arrows tipped with silver, the one metal which is deadly to our kind. They shot Una in the side, wounding her greatly.

'After the battle, we managed to get her back home where the druids took care of her as best they could. They removed the arrow, but the damage was done. Ever since that day, Una has been trapped in this form, somewhere between life and death. No one has been able to help her.'

'There must be something you can do for her?' said Cat.

'We've tried. All we can do now is make her as comfortable as we can.'

Shane tore his eyes away from the injured Una and Cat noticed they were shiny with tears.

'How can you stand it?' he said. 'Can't you hear her crying out for help?'

Domhnall looked at Shane thoughtfully. 'We can't communicate in wolf form. Not in the way we can as humans at any rate. We know she's in pain and we do what we can to ease it. We stand it because we must. When you truly love someone, you love them always, through the good times and the bad. You do not abandon them because it is hard for you to watch.'

Shane fell silent, but he didn't take his eyes off the injured she-wolf.

'How did you come to be on this island, if your home is far away?' asked Cat, seeking to change the subject.

'Now *that* is a whole other story!'

'That's enough,' came a voice from the entrance.

Domhnall appeared chastened as Conn stepped into the round house.

'Sorry,' he mumbled. 'The children had questions and—'

Conn raised a hand and cut him off. Cat thought it

was strange to see the big man cringe from the simple gesture. This Conn really did hold sway over the wolves in his care.

At the sound of Conn's voice, Una seemed to grow restless. The older man walked toward her. He crouched down and gently ran his hand over her fur. 'Hush,' he whispered, so softly Cat could barely hear. 'I'm here now.'

Una settled at his touch, falling again into sleep. Conn frowned down at her. 'She is unsettled today. Go and summon Ferdia,' he said to Domhnall.

The younger man bowed his head and shifted into his wolf form, leaving Cat and Shane alone with Conn.

'So,' said the older man, turning to regard them with those amber eyes. 'It seems you know all about me and my people. Perhaps it's time we learn more about you.'

CHAPTER FOURTEEN

The Healer

Conn gestured for Cat and Shane to sit. There was something about the older man that fascinated Cat – the way he moved with a quiet grace and spoke in a calm, measured voice. Here was a man who was used to being obeyed without question, Cat thought to herself. At first, Conn did not speak, but spent a few moments looking them both over with those strange amber eyes.

Wolf eyes, Cat thought.

Finally, he sighed and rubbed his moustache.

'You present a problem for me, children, I won't deny it. You asked Domhnall how we came to be on this island. We came here to be *safe*. For years we had to fight tooth and claw to protect our clan from harm until eventually our gods, the Tuatha Dé Danann, took pity on us and gifted us this island – a refuge of theirs that sits out of time, a place safe from the rest of the world. This island is warded by the strongest of magics. If travellers ever got close, the magic would turn them around again. No one has ever managed to breach them before, so I must ask you again – how did you manage to get through the wards?'

Cat was surprised at his words. The wards had been strong, that much was true, but how was it possible that no one but them had ever managed to break through? Maybe it was her Sight that gave them an advantage, or maybe it was the small voice in her head that urged her toward the harp, the one that refused to let her stop trying. She wasn't sure what the better answer was, but she could feel those eyes staring at her and she knew she had to say something.

'I… I don't know exactly,' said Cat, truthfully. 'I have this ability; my granny calls it the Sight. It means I can see things other people can't. I could feel the wards but … I suppose I just ignored them and kept pushing ahead.'

'Interesting,' said Conn. 'Now, the big question and answer me true, child. *Why* did you come here?'

It was now or never. Should she tell him the truth? If so, would he let them go and retrieve the harp or would he find a way to send them away from the island?

Would it be so bad if he did? she thought. *We could go home and forget all about this ridiculous quest.* As the thought crossed her mind a sharp pain once again lanced through her skull.

'Cat!' said Shane, reaching for her to steady her.

'I'm fine,' she said, brushing him off.

'Are you all right, child?' asked Conn sounding genuinely concerned.

'No, she's not. This has been happening to her all day and it seems to be getting worse,' said Shane.

'Domhnall is on his way to fetch our healer, Ferdia. I can have him take a look at you?'

'No!' Cat gasped. 'No I'm fine, honestly. I'll be OK in a minute.'

She took a breath, looked Conn in the eyes and told him the truth.

'We've come to find the Dagda's harp.'

'You've come seeking *Uaithne?*' Conn's eyes narrowed and his voice grew sharp. 'Why? Who sent you here?'

'No one sent us,' said Cat, hoping that Shane would follow her lead, but his attention was once again on injured wolf in the corner, and she couldn't tell if he was even listening to their conversation any more. 'We learned about the harp and came to get it ourselves.'

'Why would two children want the harp of power?'

'That's none of your business,' said Cat, instantly regretting her tone when Conn's eyebrows shot up in surprise. 'But I promise you that we don't mean any harm to you or to anyone,' she added. 'Please, let us go.'

Conn went silent, seemingly lost in his own thoughts. For a long time, the three of them sat around the fire, with no sound but the soft whines of Una in her fitful sleep.

Finally Conn looked up at Cat. 'These are strange times and there are powerful forces at play which I do not pretend to understand. For now, I think it is best that you stay here until I have consulted with Ferdia and the other druids about what is to be done with you.'

'You can't keep us here!' said Cat.

'I can and I will. That is my final say in the matter.'

Cat opened her mouth to plead their case some more, but went silent at the sight of Domhnall at the door with a much older man in tow. He was short and plump and walked with a slight limp. One hand rested lightly on Domhnall's arm for balance and in the other was a carved wooden staff. *This must be Ferdia,* Cat supposed.

'Well, well, what do we have here!' he said, with a smile. He had a kind face, Cat thought. 'It's been a long time indeed since we've had visitors here on the island. I hope Conn isn't giving you too much trouble.' The old man let out a wheezy laugh as he slapped Conn on the back and Cat knew for sure that she liked him. 'Now, what seems to be the problem today?'

'I will deal with the two of you in a moment,' Conn said to Cat and Shane before turning back to the healer. 'It's Una. She's restless today. I think the last draught you gave her is wearing off.'

'Already?' said Ferdia, shaking his head sadly. 'It lasted a week last time.'

'Can you give her something stronger?' asked Conn.

'That is as strong a draught as I or any of my druid

brothers know how to make. If it's no longer working…'

'Don't. Don't give up on her yet.'

'I never will,' said Ferdia, patting Conn on the arm and hobbling over to examine the wolf.

Conn looked on with worried eyes and Cat wondered how it must feel to love someone so much and have to see them in pain. She glanced at Shane and saw that he was completely absorbed in what was happening.

The old healer removed something from the pocket of his robes – a small earthen jar stoppered with cork. He popped open the cork and held the jar to the wolf's lips.

'Come on, my dear, drink up,'

Immediately, the wolf began thrashing.

'I know, I know,' said Ferdia, trying to calm her down, but still Una twisted and howled.

'Come on, children,' said Domhnall softly. 'Let us give them some privacy.'

He began guiding them out of the hut, but Shane pulled away from his grip. 'Stop!' he cried, 'Stop it! You're hurting her!'

'I know it looks that way, lad,' said Ferdia, 'But—'

'But nothing! Can't you hear her crying? She's saying

your potions aren't working any more.'

Conn looked at Shane sharply. 'What are you talking about?'

'You can hear Una speak?' asked Ferdia.

Shane looked confused, as though he were trying to pay attention to two separate conversations at once. 'Yes... I mean no. I... I don't know.'

Ferdia hauled himself to his feet and grabbed Shane by the shoulders, looking deep into his eyes.

'Concentrate, lad, for this is important. What is Una telling you?'

'I'm sorry,' Shane said. 'I can't seem to control it. I just ... when you tried to give her that potion ... it was like she was screaming at me to help but now ... now it's just noise.'

Shane looked to Cat for help.

'It's OK,' she said. 'You can do this. It's just like when I tap into the Sight. Just close your eyes and take a deep breath and it'll come to you.'

Shane nodded and did just that. For a moment, there was no sound but Una's soft whimpering. Then Shane started to speak.

'I can hear her! She… she says that she doesn't want another of Ferdia's concoctions. She says they're not doing her any good, not while the silver is still in her blood.'

Conn's head shot up and he stared at Shane. 'What? What silver? We removed the weapon years ago.'

Shane shook his head. 'No, she's saying you removed *one* of the arrows, but she had been shot twice. The second arrow broke off at the shaft and the silver-tipped arrowhead lodged itself deep in her hind leg. There … there was so much blood and pain that day … she was never able to tell you. After removing the other arrow, you stitched up her wounds and wondered why she never truly healed, why she remained stuck in her wolf form. Well, that's why. She can't change back because the silver arrowhead is still inside her and she can't heal either.'

As soon as Shane finished speaking, Conn and Ferdia began to move.

'Domhnall!' the healer called out. 'Go fetch my tools, hurry now. Conn – get the water boiling, fast as you can. Children,' he said, turning to them.

'How can we help?' asked Cat.

'You can't, but you've already done enough. Wait outside. You won't want to be here for next bit. Trust me.'

Before they could protest, Cat found herself being ushered out of the building by Ferdia's surprisingly strong
hands.

Not knowing what else to do, they stood awkwardly
around the side of the hut, waiting to see what happened
next.

'That was pretty amazing, what you did in there,' said
Cat. 'You spoke to a *wolf*! How did you even do that?'

Shane shook his head. 'I don't know. It's weird. I wasn't
actually trying to do anything. It's like she just started
talking and I happened to be the one to hear her.'

'Becca said some witches are able to talk to animals
… maybe you're a witch?' As soon as she said the words,
Cat felt a slight stab of jealousy. There was a part of her
that liked being the only one with a special ability and, as
useful as the Sight was, being able to talk to animals was
incredibly cool.

'Maybe,' said Shane doubtfully. 'This has never happened before so it's too soon to tell whether I really can
speak with animals or whether I was just able to speak
with Una. But if I can … I guess that makes me and you

a pretty unstoppable team.'

Cat relaxed a bit. However much she liked being special, she liked the idea of sharing a world of magic with her best friend just a little bit more.

'What if we just made a run for it while Conn's distracted?' said Cat.

'You can try, but it'll give me an excuse to chase you down.'

Cat groaned as Sorcha appeared before them. She was back in her human form again and looking every bit as surly as earlier.

'What are you two doing out here?' she asked. 'I thought I told you to wait inside.'

'Conn sent us out,' said Shane. 'Ferdia needs to perform some emergency surgery on Una, and I guess they didn't want us getting in the way.'

'What do you mean? What's wrong with Una?'

'Nothing that hasn't been wrong for her for who knows how long,' said Cat. 'And I would speak to us with a bit more respect if I were you since it's thanks to Shane here that Ferdia has a chance of healing Una once and for all.'

Sorcha glared at them and then, to Cat's surprise, spat

on the ground in front of them.

'You think I should speak to you with respect? Tell me, why is it on the very day when our druids predict a great power rising again, the two of you show up on this island? You expect me to believe that is a coincidence?'

Cat furrowed her brow. 'What do you mean, "a great power rising"?'

'It means we are preparing for war, little girl. And when battle commences, you had better hope that you are on the right side of it.'

War. The word sent chills down Cat's spine. So that was why the clan seemed to be preparing such a large supply of weapons.

That can't be anything to do with us, Cat thought. *We're just kids. It has to be a coincidence.*

She wanted to ask Sorcha more, but just then Conn appeared at the entrance way. His face was grave.

'Is everything OK?' asked Shane. 'What happened with Una?'

'She is resting. Come, children. I believe we have more to discuss.'

CHAPTER FIFTEEN

Leave Taking

Conn led Cat and Shane away from the hut where Una slept and brought them instead to a smaller, one-room building. It too was made of wood and reeds, but it was much more sparsely furnished than the last. It contained little more than a raised bed covered in sheepskin blankets, two long wooden benches and a small fire pit with a bundle of wood stacked neatly beside it. It was a practical space, where everything had a function and a place. In short, it was a room fit for a warrior who needed to be ready at a moment's notice. Conn gestured for them to sit.

'How is she?' asked Shane, taking his place on one of

the benches. 'I could hear her for a while but then she went quiet, and I was worried.'

Conn smiled at him, and it was the first time Cat had seen his face anything other than serious.

'She's doing well, lad. Thanks to you. She is back in human form now for the first time in … well, in far too long. She's resting.'

'Will she be OK?' asked Cat.

The smile slipped from Conn's face. 'We don't know. She's weak right now so it is hard to say for certain what may happen, but Ferdia says that she was sick for so long there is a chance she may never fully recover.'

'There has to be something more we can do!' said Shane, looking devastated.

Conn shook his head. 'We can't heal everyone, much as we may wish to. Our job is to do our best for the people we love and be there for them when they need us.'

'But—'

'No buts, lad. You'll drive yourself mad trying to find some way to magic it all better – believe me, I know.'

'Then we didn't really help at all,' said Shane and Cat knew him well enough to know he was holding back tears.

'You made the world of difference!' said Conn. 'You heard her, and you understood her. That matters more than you can ever know. After all these years, Una is finally comfortable and for that, I owe you a great debt.'

Shane said nothing but Cat could see the pain written all over his face as clear as day. That was strange. Sure, it was sad that Una might never get better, and it must have been worse for Shane to actually hear how much pain she was in, but they didn't even know her. Why was he so shaken by the news? Cat resolved to ask him about it later, once they were away from the wolf village.

'Please,' she said, turning to Conn. 'Please let us go now. Surely you can see that we don't mean you or anyone any harm? Let us make our way to the fort and we'll be off the island as soon as we have the harp.'

Conn sighed. 'It wasn't for fear you'd harm anyone that we kept you here, girl. There were … other factors to consider.'

'Is this about the "great power" that's supposed to arise? Because honestly that doesn't have anything to do with us.'

'I would not be so sure about that,' said a voice from the

173

doorway. Cat turned just as Ferdia limped into the hut, once again leaning on Domhnall's arm for support. Conn pulled a pallet over for the old man to sit down on, which he did with a grateful smile.

'Thank you, Conn, these old bones aren't what they were. So, my girl,' he said, folding his hands under his chin and turning his attention to Cat. 'I hear you've come here seeking *Uaithne.*'

'Yes, but—'

'Ah, now, don't interrupt. Let me say my piece.'

Cat blushed. She couldn't help but like the old man and she didn't mean to be rude.

'Now then, where was I? Oh, yes. Conn has invited me here to speak to you because it was I who read the signs in the runes. There is a great power that is about to awaken. An ancient evil who seeks to come to full power. Tell me, child, who was it who sent you here?'

'I already told Conn; we weren't sent by anyone.'

'Are you sure?'

Doubt flashed across Cat's mind. Becca had told her of this place, but it had been her idea to come here, hadn't it?

'Will you do an old man a favour, girl?' asked Ferdia.

Cat nodded.

'All right, look into my eyes for just a moment.'

Cat did. She found the old man's eyes to be remarkably clear. After a moment, he gave a slight frown and sat back onto the pallet, lost in thought.

'You have a part to play in things,' he said, eventually. 'Though I cannot tell what shape that takes. There are many things that are hidden from me.' Then he turned to Conn and said, 'Let them go. They are bound up in the hands of fate and we are in no position to stop them.'

Conn nodded and stood up. 'Come, children, and I will escort you to the village boundary.'

Cat thanked Ferdia profusely and was surprised at how sad the old man looked. 'Take care,' was all he said in return.

Conn walked them through the huts to where the path sloped up again toward the mountaintop. On the way, they passed more members of the tribe and all of them seemed grave.

'Sorcha said you are preparing for battle,' said Cat. 'Are you that sure something bad is about to happen?'

'Nothing in life is ever certain, but it's best to be prepared.'

When they passed the last hut, Conn stopped. 'This is where I leave you. Though I do not believe that you should be undertaking this quest, I trust Ferdia when he tells me you have a part to play in the events that are about to unfold. All I ask is that you be careful on your journey. The fortress where *Uaithne* rests is a cursed place.'

'We can handle—' Cat started to plead, but was silenced by Conn's raised hand.

'You do not understand. When the Tuatha Dé Danann returned to the Otherworld they left behind a guardian to protect the treasures they couldn't take with them.'

'What kind of guardian?' asked Cat.

'An old being. A demon of the air. We do not venture close to the fort and in turn the demon leaves us in peace, but every so often, we hear reports from wolves on patrol of a darkness that seems to follow them and watch their every move.'

Cat felt her blood turn to ice. A demon of the air... there was something about that. Something familiar. She wished she had her Book of Secrets with her to reference. Although, she reminded herself, if she had brought it, it would have ended up at the bottom of the sea along with her schoolbag.

'Thank you for the warning,' said Cat. 'We'll be careful, I promise.'

'We still owe you a debt, for helping Una,' said Conn. 'Do not think I have forgotten that. If there is a way for us to repay you, send word and if it is within our power, it will be done.' With that, he turned and made his way back to the village. Back to Una.

Throughout the whole exchange, Shane never said a word. He simply stared at the ground with a glazed look in his eye.

Cat gave his sleeve a soft tug and he seemed to snap back into focus.

'Come on,' she said, gently. 'It's time to go.'

* * *

Shane knew his feet were moving but his mind was a million miles away. He was only vaguely aware of his surroundings as he and Cat left the wolf village behind and made for the fortress that sat high above them. The first part of the hike was tough going, the well-worn trails of the wolf tribe gave way to steep inclines with lots of loose rocks that threatened to trip them up. Cat kept trying to make light-hearted conversation, but all Shane could think of was Una and how much she reminded him of his mother.

He knew their situations weren't the same, obviously, but in a strange way he felt like they were connected. They had both suffered in silence for a long time and the people who loved them could only look on and hope that one day things would get better. But what if they didn't?

He had set out on this mission wishing he could find some way to make his mother better once and for all, but something Conn said kept nagging at him. *'We can't heal everyone, much as we may wish to. Our job is to do our best for the people we love and be there for them when they need us.'*

Was using magic on her cheating somehow? Was it wrong? Conn said that you could drive yourself mad trying to magic away your problems, and wasn't that exactly what he was trying to do? All these questions swirled around his head until he felt something like panic rising in his chest.

'... and now that you have this new ability to talk to

animals, maybe that means Becca will train us both!' Cat said, totally oblivious to the internal battle raging within Shane. 'Wouldn't that be cool? We could be like super heroes! Me with my Sight and you with—'

'Stop!' said Shane, clutching the side of his head as though he could make his thoughts slow down. 'Just stop a second, Cat, please.'

She looked at him with concern, 'Are you OK?' she asked. 'You look a little freaked out.'

'I am freaked out! Aren't you?'

'A little, I guess…'

'A little?' Shane was yelling now, but he couldn't stop himself. All at once this whole quest seemed so absurd to him. 'We were just taken prisoner by *wolves* and there's some kind of *demon* in that castle… why are we even *doing* this?'

'We're getting the harp for Becca.'

'Right, for Becca. Why does Becca even want the harp?'

'We've been over this Shane; she's using it in her research.'

'But her research is into holy wells, remember? She told us the first day we met her. What does a magical harp belonging to one of the Tuatha Dé Danann have to do with that?'

Shane had her there; he could see Cat's forehead furrow in confusion.

'What do we really know about Becca anyway? For all we know, she could be some kind of supervillain who's planning to use the harp to take over the world.'

'Don't be silly,' said Cat. 'Becca's nice.'

Shane tugged at his hair in exasperation, why wasn't Cat getting this?

'She may be nice, but the harp *isn't*.'

'What do you mean?'

'I don't know. It's just … none of this feels *right*. I keep thinking about what Conn said back there, about loving people as they are no matter what. Say the harp does work, and I use it to make my mam happy again. It won't be *real*, will it? And what if it doesn't last? What if she's happy for like a week and then it wears off and we're right back where we started? Do I need to keep using the harp on her over and over again forever? Maybe Conn's right. Maybe we do just have to love the people in our lives the way they are. And…' Shane paused, sure that what he was about to say was going to cross a line.

'And what?' Cat demanded.

'And maybe that goes for you too. Maybe you just have to accept your mam just as she is, even if that means accepting her new boyfriend too.'

Shane expected Cat to yell at him. Instead, her whole body seemed to sag. She opened her mouth to say something, but then gasped and clutched her head. Her face was a picture of agony.

'Cat!' he yelled, rushing to her side. 'What's going on?'

She took several gulping breaths, trying to steady herself.

'I ... don't know,' she gasped. 'It's like, whenever I think about what we're doing, I get this blinding pain in my head.'

Cat let out another cry and Shane could see that her eyes were wet with tears.

'There's something wrong, please, let's just go home. We'll go to your granny and—'

'No!' Cat yelled, pushing Shane back. 'You don't understand, Shane, I *can't* go back. You're right, there *is* something wrong, but whatever it is won't be fixed until I get the harp.'

'That doesn't make any sense! Come *on*, Cat.'

Cat looked at him with such sadness, he felt his heart break all over again. How had he not seen this sooner? He knew her behaviour wasn't right, but he just pushed it down and ignored it for his own selfish reasons.

'OK,' she said finally. 'You're right, let's go.' She pulled the Clurichaun's cap out of her pocket and Shane felt his whole body relax. They'd be back in Clonbridge soon and Cat's granny would know exactly how to fix her. He reached for her hand just as the Clurichaun instructed.

'I'm sorry,' said Cat, and before Shane could react, she placed the cap in his hand and shoved him away yelling, 'Clurichaun! Take Shane home.'

Shane's eyes widened in horror as he felt the fairy's magic pull him back home, away from Cat.

In the blink of an eye, he found himself standing by the wall to Granny's back garden. The very place they had left from that morning. The Clurichaun was in front of him, bent double and wheezing slightly, 'It worked!' he said with a chuckle. 'I've never done that before, and I wasn't sure I could get ye both from such a distance...'

He straightened and his wrinkled face fell in horror when he saw that it was Shane alone clutching his cap. 'Where's Caitriona?'

'She … she stayed behind.' The realisation of what Cat had just done finally dawned on Shane. He rushed over to the Clurichaun and grabbed him by the shoulders. 'We have to go back for her!'

'I'm sorry, but—'

'Hurry! Just put me back exactly where I was. She can't have gotten far.'

'I told you, I *can't do that*, lad,' said the Clurichaun sadly. 'You know I can't cross the wards. We'd have to go back to the shore and find another boat and then you'd have to cross the wards yourself.'

'But there's no time for that,' said Shane. 'There's something wrong with Cat and we have to help her.'

'What do you mean something's wrong with the girl? Is she hurt?'

'No,' said Shane. 'She's not hurt, but … I don't know what it is.'

Suddenly, from out of the long grass a tiny, furry face appeared. Shane jumped in surprise when Vinnie the stoat scurried up his leg and onto his shoulder.

'I think I might know…' he said.

CHAPTER SIXTEEN

Vinnie's Search

Vinnie had been searching for Cat for hours and was beginning to despair, when he finally caught a familiar whiff and followed her scent right to her front door. He did a little jig of happiness.

Hold on, Becca! he thought. *Help is on the way!* His next problem was finding a way to speak with Cat. She wouldn't be able to understand him, he knew, but if he could only get in front of her, he would surely be able to figure something out. It was late by the time he got there, and all the doors and windows were shut tight for the night. He scaled the drainpipe and plopped himself onto the first windowsill he saw. He peered in through a small gap in the curtain and there she was, fast asleep on her bed. He began to squeak and scrabble furiously against the glass, but it was no use. She couldn't hear him.

He was tired himself now. It had been a long and stressful day. Normally, the life of a familiar was a relatively cushy one. He had someone to feed him and house him and ensure that he had nice warm bed to curl up in at night. He hadn't lived on his own in the outdoors for a very long time and he was scared. He also missed Becca. The bond between a witch and her familiar was a strong one. She was his best friend and being without her was painful. He hoped that she was all right.

He felt tiredness take over and reluctantly he made his way back down the drainpipe to find some safe space where he could sleep. He would find Cat first thing in the morning, he decided. He'd figure out a way to let her know about the *geas* she was under and then, once they found a way around it, they would save Becca together. He found a small dry hole and curled his body tight to him before drifting off to sleep.

It was bright when he woke. Too bright. He had slept much longer than he intended. With a start, he leapt from his burrow and straight away he caught a hint of the girl's scent. She was already gone and was probably in school by now. How could he have slept in so late!

Without even a thought of finding breakfast, Vinnie set out on their trail. Cat's scent was soon joined by the boy's but to Vinnie's surprise, they didn't head off toward town as he expected. He traced it through the estate and into the fields that lay beyond. He followed it right up the wall of a farmhouse where it suddenly disappeared.

That can't be right, he thought.

He turned around in circles, searching for another hint of where they might have gone but there was nothing. It was as though they had vanished into thin air. Suddenly, he caught a whiff of something else. He sniffed deeply. There was magic in the air. Not like Becca's magic which felt warm and welcoming and not like the ancient, raw power he felt when Cethlenn took over Becca's body. This was something else. Fairy magic. He bit his little stoat lip and pondered his next move. Fairies were tricky creatures, but they did have a fondness for nature and animals. Better than that – fairies could *understand* animals. Maybe if he could find this fairy, he could ask it for help with Becca?

He was running through all the different scenarios in his head when a few things happened very quickly. Out of thin air, a short, bald man appeared, and Vinnie let out a yelp and dived into a patch of long grass. He peeked out and watched as the fairy man closed his eyes tight as if he were concentrating and mumbled something to himself. A second later, another figure appeared. It was the boy, but he seemed distressed. He began shaking the fairy man and telling him that there was something wrong with Cat and they had to go back for her.

Vinnie couldn't wait any longer. He burst out of his hiding place and scurried up Shane's leg.

'I think I might know...' he said.

Shane yelped and almost flung Vinnie off, but the stoat held on tight.

'Oh, it's just you,' he said, his voice shaky. 'You have to stop jumping on me!'

'Ah, lad, there's a stoat on your shoulder,' said the fairy.

'I know!' said Shane, who seemed annoyed. 'What are you doing here?' He craned his head to try and look and Vinnie. 'And what do you mean you know what's wrong with Cat?'

'You can hear me!' Vinnie said.

'Yes, but we don't have time to get into that now,' said Shane. 'Tell us what's wrong with Cat!'

Vinnie squeaked and launched into the full explanation. He told them all about Becca being possessed and about the *geas* she put on Cat.

Shane frowned at him. 'I'm sorry, I … this whole speaking with animals thing is new to me and I don't fully understand what you just said.'

'I do,' said the Clurichaun. 'And it's not good. Caitriona has been placed under a *geas* by an ancient being that's currently possessing the body of your witch friend!'

'A *geas*?' said Shane. 'Is that like a spell?'

'Not exactly,' said the Clurichaun. 'How can I explain … a *geas* is a kind of obligation. If someone is placed under a *geas* it means they *have to* follow it no matter what.'

Shane slapped his forehead. 'That's why Cat is so determined to get the harp! Any time she even thought about giving up it caused her pain.'

'That would be part of it,' said the Clurichaun.

'So we just break the *geas*, right? Then she'll be back to

normal?'

The Clurichaun looked directly at Vinnie who began to squirm.

'What's going on?' said Shane. 'Why that look?'

'You need to tell him,' said Vinnie to the fairy.

'It's not that simple lad, a *geas* is not something that can just be broken. There are … consequences. If Cat has been ordered to bring back the harp then she has to do it or…'

'Or she'll die,' said Vinnie. He knew that Shane understood him fully this time because the colour drained from the boy's face, leaving his freckles to stand out against his pale skin. 'And there's a very real chance Becca will die too unless we can find a way to help her!' added Vinnie. 'Her spirit is fading fast. We need to do something.'

Shane closed his eyes and rubbed his temple. 'OK. We need to find a way to help both Cat and Becca and I don't think we can do it alone. We need to find Cat's granny, she's our only hope.'

The Clurichaun nodded. 'She'll be at Caitriona's house by now.'

'Then what are we waiting for? Let's go!'

CHAPTER SEVENTEEN

Demon of the Air

Cat wondered what time it was and whether school would be finished by now. Cat thought it must be early afternoon by now, but it was hard to tell. The sky had clouded over, and the island felt dark and lonely. She almost regretted sending Shane away, but she knew it had been the right thing to do. Shane was right – something *was* wrong and even though Cat didn't know exactly what that was, she knew that she couldn't drag Shane into it any more than she already had. She tried her best to put it out of her mind and keep walking.

The trail up to the fort grew ever steeper and Cat had to be careful about where she placed her feet to avoid sliding back down the hill on the loose shale.

Finally, after about half an hour of hiking, she crested the hill and found herself face to face with an ancient fortress. It was bigger than she anticipated, spanning about half the length of her school's sports field and it formed an almost perfect circle. The walls were made of rough-hewn grey stone that had been weathered and worn by centuries of Atlantic wind and rain. They towered over Cat and though she was too short to see, she believed the fort was open to the sky.

There was no opening that Cat could see – not even a narrow slit for the fort's defenders to look out of. She frowned and headed to the left, searching for a gate or even a hole in the wall she could squeeze through. Her search came to an abrupt end when the ground gave way to high cliff face that loomed over the sea far below. Cat gasped and stumbled backwards, feeling dizzy at the sight. She hadn't realised how high she had climbed.

She retraced her steps and tried following the wall the opposite way, but was soon faced with the same situation – the wall bent around unbroken until it met the cliff edge.

Cat wondered what she should do next. It was too high to climb, and she didn't have any rope that could help her along the way. Besides, the stones of the wall were stacked together so expertly she doubted she could fit a razor blade between the cracks, let alone find a finger hold.

She sat down on a nearby rock and wondered what to do next. She knew this was the right place: she could feel the magic of the harp down to her bones. There *had* to be a way to get in. She stared out over the ocean. In the distance, she could see the wall of mist and Cat thought how difficult this place must have been for enemies to attack – between the wards, the towering cliffs on one side, and the long steep climb up to the fort on the other, it was no wonder the Tuatha Dé Danann chose this place to hide their treasures when they retreated to the Otherworld. How had she ever thought she would be able to get past the defences by herself? Cat curled her arms around herself and tried not to cry.

A shadow fell across her eye line and Cat realised she wasn't alone. There was someone else here in this lonely place. Someone high above, watching her.

She looked up and saw something perched on top of

the wall, staring down at her. At first she thought it was a large crow or raven because it had jet black feathers and what looked like a long, pointed beak. As it spread its wings and pulled itself up to its full height, Cat realised in horror that it was no bird, but the guardian of the fort, the demon of the air that Conn had warned her of. She leapt off the rock and tried to run. If she could get back to the wolf village, surely they would help her? But no matter how hard she tried, she couldn't get her legs to move.

This is no time to run, said the voice in her head. *Not when the harp is so close!*

So she remained, frozen in horror, as the creature above her sprang from the wall and glided toward her with an unnatural grace.

'Who goes there?' said the creature in a voice that sounded to Cat like a fork scraping across a china plate. 'Who dares disturb the ancient fort of Hy-Brasil?'

Cat wanted to scream and part of her still wanted to run, but she knew if she did that the pain in her head would overwhelm her. She was trapped and so her only hope was to try and reason with the demon. So she gritted her teeth and began to speak.

'I'm here to retrieve *Uaithne*, the harp of the Dagda.'

The demon swooped in circles above Cat's head, occasionally diving close enough for her to see the creature's bright yellow eyes. It was a horrible thing, though its body was indeed covered with feathers, its wings were more like that of a bat – thin and leathery and ending in long, hooked claws.

'Why do you seek the harp of power little one? Be truthful now, I will know if you lie.'

'My friend wants it. She's a witch.'

'A witch, you say? There were people who called me such, a long time ago now. But that is not the full truth. Tell me why you seek *Uaithne*.'

'I told you—'

'You told me what you wanted me to hear,' said the demon, this time dipping so low, Cat could feel the creature's claws rake through her hair. 'But there is something more you are hiding. This is your last chance, child. Why do you want the harp?'

'I…' Cat hesitated, ashamed of what she was about to say. 'I want to use it on my mother to make her fall out of love with her new boyfriend.'

THE HARP OF POWER

'Why?'

'Because she shouldn't be with him… because things were fine the way they were. We were a team – me, Mam, and Mikey. We don't need anyone else.'

The demon came to land right in front of Cat and extended to its full height. She cowered away from it.

For a moment the creature said nothing, but regarded Cat with those beady yellow eyes. Finally, it spoke.

'You have met the wolves.' It was not a question, but still Cat nodded. 'They will have told you of the prophecy.'

Again, Cat nodded. How did this creature know about that?

As if reading her mind, it answered. 'I see and hear many things, living as I do among the wind and shadows. I have heard the rumblings among the druids of the wolf clan that a great and terrible power is about to rise. They are worried, and they are right to be. I have my own ways of divining the future and what I have seen tells the same story. A powerful force will indeed return to this land.'

'I don't see what that has to do with me,' said Cat, defiantly.

'Ah but you do, because the wolf seer also told you

that you have a part to play in the coming events,' said the demon who was closer to Cat now, so close that it reached out with one of its claw-tipped wings and brushed a strand of Cat's hair away from her face. 'What he didn't tell you was that your part will be dictated by the actions you take on this very day. I could put an end to the prophecy right now if I wanted,' continued the demon. 'It would not take much effort. You are such a small thing…'

Cat took a step backwards, but she was close to the cliff edge – too close. One misstep would have her falling to her doom.

'Please,' said Cat and her voice was thin. 'Don't hurt me.'

Cat could have sworn that the demon smiled at her.

'Do not worry, Caitriona Donnelly. I have had enough death and destruction to last a lifetime. Besides, once the threads of prophecy are woven, there is no stopping them, however much we might wish to. All we can do is hope for the best.'

'How do you know my name?' asked Cat.

'I know many things. More than you can imagine. You have done well to get this far, Caitriona. There are many who have come to Hy-Brasil over the centuries in search of the Dagda's treasures and not all of them have fared so well. You have already proven yourself a worthy character and if you can find the entrance the fort, I will offer you what aid I can.'

Before Cat could say another word, the demon shot upward, circled her once and then flew over the wall, into the heart of the stone fort.

Cat felt her knees go weak and she slumped back down onto the rock to think. Why had the demon spared her? And what did it mean that it knew more than she could imagine. She chewed her thumbnail thoughtfully. It had also said it would help her ... did she want the kind of help a demon could offer? She wasn't sure. But she needed to get in there one way or another regardless.

'If you can find the entrance', Cat thought. *That was what the demon said. That must mean there* is *a way to get in.*

But she had already walked the full length of the wall without seeing an opening, unless...

Unless it can't be seen!

Cat shot to her feet again. She knew why she couldn't find the entrance – it was glamoured, hidden by magic.

She wished she had remembered to bring the hagstone with her. It was currently sitting in her drawer at home along with the Book of Secrets and her other treasures. She had been given the stone on Halloween by a ghost and had been able to use it to find her way out of the Green Rath. She was sure that it could have broken through this glamour right away. Instead, she would have to rely on her Sight to tell her where the entrance was hidden.

She closed her eyes, took a deep breath to steady herself, and tapped into the Sight. She opened her eyes again and waited for the familiar pull of magic. It was difficult to tell – the whole place was teeming with magic. The very stones of the hill were singing with power. She had to sift through it all until she felt what she believed to be the glamour. It was faint, but it was there. She began following the spell around the wall, feeling it grow ever stronger as she got closer and closer. Finally, when she was sure she was in the right place, she reached forward and pressed her hands against the stone. But it wasn't stone she felt there. It was wood – the wood of a gate that swung open at her touch, revealing a wide-open courtyard and in the centre of it, the demon.

'Well done,' said the demon, and before Cat could respond, it transformed from a wretched creature of feather and scale into a woman, young and beautiful. She looked weary and a little sad. 'Hello Caitriona. My name is Aoife, welcome to my home.'

'Um, hi,' she replied, a familiar feeling tugging at her. Aoife … a demon of the air … there was something vaguely familiar about all of this. Something that she should already know.

Then it hit her. 'Wait a second, you're Aoife? *The* Aoife? Aoife as in, the wicked stepmother who turned the Children of Lir into swans?'

Aoife raised her eyebrow slightly and Cat blushed.

Oh, no! Did I just call her a wicked stepmother? she thought. *She's totally going to turn back into that demon and claw my eyes out!*

Thankfully, Aoife just smiled at her. 'Well, I'm glad to hear my reputation precedes me. Come, Caitriona, we have much to discuss.'

With that she turned and made her way across the courtyard toward a long stone building that sat in the very centre of the fort.

Cat hesitated; she had grown up listening to Granny tell her stories about the Children of Lir. She knew that that this woman was a powerful sorceress who had cursed her husband's children to live as swans for nine hundred years and was, in turn, transformed into a demon as punishment for her crime.

Could she trust Aoife?

Did she even have a choice?

Almost there, she told herself. *Just keep your wits about you.*

With that, she took a deep breath and followed Aoife.

CHAPTER EIGHTEEN

Aoife's Tale

As she stepped into the courtyard, Cat couldn't help but notice how different it was from the wolf village. There, everything felt warm and lived in, but this fortress felt like a ghost town.

'Are you the only one who lives here?' asked Cat as she followed Aoife up the stairs that led up to the large central building.

'Yes,' Aoife replied and though her back was to her, Cat could hear the sadness in her voice. 'I am alone.'

She pushed open the heavy wooden door and gestured for Cat to go ahead of her. Cat took a breath and stepped inside.

The inside of the stone building was dark. The only light came from flaming torches that were set into the wall. For a second Cat felt her heart constrict because it reminded her of Halloween night when she and Shane had entered the fairy fort in search of their siblings. That time, the way out had disappeared behind them, but a quick glance over her shoulder confirmed that the door was still there.

Together, they walked down the narrow corridor and through another door that led into a great hall. Two long wooden tables ran down the length of the hall with enough room to fit a hundred people around them Cat thought. Three of walls were covered in colourful tapestries depicting battles and feasts and for some reason, the fourth wall was left bare. She didn't have time to wonder why because her attention was soon drawn to large stone fire pit in the centre of the hall over which sat a large stew pot. The fire was lit, and the most wonderful smells filled the hall. Cat felt her tummy rumble; she had eaten nothing for hours other than a few polite bites of bread at the wolf village. Aoife must have heard it too because she asked if Cat would like some stew.

'It's safe, I promise. You are a guest here and no harm will be done.'

That had been true in the wolf village, but this was Aoife, the woman who cursed her own stepchildren. Wasn't she one of the bad guys?

'I understand that you do not trust me, but I am not one of the *Sídhe*, looking to steal you away. There is no enchanted food here,' said Aoife. 'Besides, as you so rightly noticed, I could have thrown you from the cliffs if I had wanted to harm you.'

Aoife gestured for Cat to take a seat while she ladled them up a bowl each. Hunger won out and Cat took a small sip. The stew was warm and delicious.

'Did you make this?' she asked, wondering how Aoife could possibly get all the ingredients living here all alone.

Aoife shook her head. 'When the Tuatha Dé Danann left me here to guard this stronghold, they did not leave me entirely without help. The Dagda himself set a charm to ensure that the larder is always full of fresh bread and mead and that the stew pot never grows empty. I have everything I need here.'

They sat in silence for a while as they ate. Finally, Aoife

pushed her bowl away and stared at Cat over folded hands.

'Look at me for a moment,' she said, leaning forward and grasping Cat's chin in her hand. Cat wanted to pull back, but Aoife held her in place with gentle force. She locked eyes with Aoife and felt a subtle force probing at her mind. After what felt like an eternity, Aoife finally let go. Cat thought she looked troubled.

'It is as I thought,' she muttered.

'What's as you thought?' said Cat.

Aoife pursed her lips. 'I must tell you something, Caitriona, but before I do, I need you to trust me. I know that is no easy task for you. You know who I am and what I have done – or at least you think you do. Let me tell you some of my story in my own words and then you can decide if you believe what I will tell you next.

'It is true that I am the Aoife of legend and that I have done many terrible and wicked things … I was young when I married Lir, a man much older than me who had been married before to my own sister. After she died, I was heartbroken. I found myself married to her widower and in charge of her four young children. I wished nothing more than to be a good wife to Lir and a good step-mother to his children, but grief can make you do strange things.

'Lir had loved my sister – how could he not? She was beautiful and kind, all the things I am not. After her death, he doted on the children, especially his only daughter, Fionnuala, who looked so like my sister. They were the last piece of her he had left. I see that now. But at the time, I felt as though I had been cast aside. I was convinced that he would never love me, not while he was constantly reminded of the woman who had been better than I in every way.'

Granny had told Cat the story of the Children of Lir countless times, but this was the first time Cat ever thought about it from Aoife's point of view and she was surprised to find that she understood where Aoife was coming from.

'I thought that if we could just have some time alone together, he would learn to love me,' she continued. 'And in my desperation, I did something unforgivable – I cursed the children to live as swans for many hundreds of years. The second I cast the spell, I was filled with regret.

I would have taken it back in a heartbeat if I could, but even I did not possess that power. Not then. When I was turned into a demon of the air, I gladly accepted my punishment.

'For hundreds of years I roamed the earth. At first, I followed the children as they moved from lake to sea, keeping an eye on them from afar, though they never knew I was there. When the nine hundred years were up, their curse was broken, and they were returned to human form, but I was still trapped in my demon body. Eventually, the Tuatha Dé Danann showed me some mercy – more than I had ever shown for my sister's children. More than I deserved. When the time came for them to retreat to the Otherworld, they agreed to break the curse on me if I in turn agreed to stay behind and guard their treasures here on this island out of time until they returned to finally release me from my penance.'

'And they haven't come back?' said Cat realising that she was stating the obvious as soon as the words were out of her mouth.

'They have not. But I have hope and so I remain here alone with my regrets.' She paused and her beautiful face was so sad, Cat couldn't help but feel some sympathy for her. She had done something terrible, but did she deserve to be punished like this?

'Do you know what I learned over the many long years I have spent on this island, Caitriona?'

Cat shook her head.

'I've learned that my biggest mistake was doubting the human heart. We have so much capacity for love Caitriona, and new love does not push away the old. The human heart expands to make room for it all. If I had given Lir time to mourn, if I had truly given myself time to mourn, then maybe...' Aoife left the sentence hanging in the air, but Cat knew what she had been about to say – *then maybe things would have been different.*

They sat in silence for a moment and Cat found herself replaying Aoife's words in her mind – *new love does not push away the old.* Wasn't that exactly what she herself was worried about? The second her mother told her about Darren, all she could think about was how her mother wouldn't have time for her any more. But what if that wasn't true at all? What if there was room in her mother's heart for them all?

'Don't be like me Caitriona,' Aoife said finally, breaking into Cat's thoughts. 'Don't do something you will regret.'

'What you do you mean?' Cat said. 'If you're telling me not to take the harp then—'

'No, I know you must take the harp,' Aoife replied. 'I wish I could keep it from you, keep you safe, but … do you know what I saw when I looked in your eyes?'

Cat was confused, what was she talking about? She shook her head.

'You've been placed under a *geas,* girl. Do you know what that is?'

Cat felt her heart skip a beat. She did indeed know what a *geas* was. Granny had told her all about them, but how could that possibly be? Who would have done that to her? She had so many questions but the first one that came to mind was, 'What kind of *geas*?'

'A bad one,' Aoife said. 'One that I cannot break, much as I would like to.'

'I don't understand…' said Cat and Aoife smiled at her sadly.

'You will. I cannot break your *geas*, but I can help you see it for yourself. Give me your hand.'

Before Cat could ask any more questions, Aoife took her hand in hers. She whispered some words and then—

Suddenly it all became clear. Cat remembered the dark shadow that had been stalking Becca. The change that had come over her when Cat tried to leave. The way Vinnie had disappeared. She remembered the story Becca had told her, about the battle between the Tuatha Dé Danann and the Fomorians. And she recalled the way Becca had spoken the words that had sealed her fate. *I place this geas on you – you will travel across the waves to Hy-Brasil and seek out the guardian of the harp. You will take it from her and then return the harp to me. If you fail to do this, your life will be forfeit.*

But it wasn't Becca who had said those words, was it? It was something else. Someone else… Someone who had stolen Becca's body and manipulated Cat into getting the harp on her behalf.

'Her name is Cethlenn,' said Aoife softly.

Cethlenn, of course. The Fomorian queen whose husband had been killed by the Tuatha Dé Danann. It all made so much sense now! She finally understood why she had woken up with a burning desire to get the harp;

why every time she or Shane had questioned the sense of going on this quest, she was struck with blinding pain; why, when she knew in heart it was wrong, she had kept going.

Your life will be forfeit. The words ricocheted around her brain. Was she going to die?

When she came to her senses, she found that she was bent over double, gasping for air and Aoife was gently rubbing her back.

'Deep breaths, Caitriona. All will be well.'

'How can you say that?' she cried, feeling her eyes welling with tears. 'If I don't take the harp I'll die and if I do…'

Another part of the mystery clicked into place: the wolves' prophecy. The great power rising. Ferdia telling her she had a part to play… Sorcha had been right to distrust her: she was the reason all of this was happening. Cat couldn't hold it in any longer. She began to cry.

'Hush now,' said Aoife, her voice soft and soothing. 'This is not your fault.'

'But it *is*!' Cat said, her voice ragged. 'The only reason I was over at Becca's that day was because I was still mad at my mam for having a boyfriend and didn't want to go home and face her. I told Becca all about it and I suppose Cethlenn heard too. I even said I wished things could go back to the way they were. I said I wished she would just fall out of love with Darren. I said that! And if I hadn't … if I hadn't been so selfish, maybe it wouldn't have been so easy to put a *geas* on me … to make me feel like this was all my own idea.'

'Caitriona,' said Aoife, her voice suddenly serious. 'I need you to listen to me. You are human. It is in your nature to be selfish sometimes. Your thoughts and feelings do not make you a bad person, it's what you do about them that matters.'

Cat thought back to Aoife's words – *Don't be like me, Caitriona. Don't do something you will regret.*

She was right – Shane was right. Cat could never – *would* never – use the harp to change her mother's feelings for Darren, no matter how hurt she felt. She had to trust that Aoife was right and that her mother's heart was big enough for all of them.

Cat dried her eyes. There was still the matter of what was to happen next. Even though she had no intention of using it herself, she still had to get the harp and bring it to Cethlenn, otherwise she would die. But if she did that then Cethlenn would have one of the most powerful tools in existence in her possession. What would a Fomorian queen do with such a weapon? Cat shuddered to think.

Cat said as much to Aoife who nodded at her. 'Yes,' she said. 'It is quite the predicament we find ourselves in, but perhaps … perhaps there is a way for everything to come good in the end. I will give you the harp Caitriona and you must take it to Cethlenn as promised … but who is to say that you must bring it to her directly?'

'What do you mean?'

'There are things that I can perhaps set in motion, but we need some time. Do you have somewhere safe?' Aoife asked, 'Somewhere you can take the harp until help arrives?'

Cat nodded. She knew exactly where to go.

'Then let us waste no more time. Come, Caitriona, let me show you the treasures of the Tuatha Dé Danann.'

Aoife stood and walked to the back of the hall, to the one wall that had been left unadorned. She waved her hand and suddenly the wall shimmered and where bare stone had been just a moment before was a collection of the most fascinating treasures Cat had ever seen. She stepped closer, examining them. There were goblets and plates of various metals, shields with beautiful designs painted on them, and there, mounted in pride of place, were the three treasures of the Dagda. The spear, the cauldron, and the harp.

Cat could feel the power rippling off them like waves.

Aoife reached out and pulled the harp free from the wall and handed it to Cat. She was surprised at how heavy it was, for such a small instrument.

'Won't you get in trouble with the Tuatha Dé Danann for giving away one of their treasures?' She asked.

'Perhaps,' Aoife replied, 'But I will accept whatever punishment comes my way, just as I have always done. Now come. We must get you home.'

Cat's heart sank. She had sent Shane away with the Clurichaun's cap. She had no idea how she would get off this island.

'Do not worry,' Aoife said when she told her. 'I have a way.'

She led Cat back out of the great hall and down a

different corridor that opened out into the back of the courtyard. There, roped to a pillar, was the most beautiful horse Cat had ever seen. Its coat was so white it seemed to glow silver and the fading afternoon sunlight danced off its long, flowing mane. She could feel the horse's power even from across the courtyard.

'This is Énbarr. He belonged to the sea god Manannán. He was also left in my care when his master returned to the Otherworld.'

Aoife ran a pale hand over the horse's nose, and he gave a soft huff of pleasure. 'He was born to ride across the waves, and he will see you home safely.'

Aoife helped Cat onto the horse's back. She expected him to buck and rear, but he was gentle and kept perfectly still for her.

Aoife led them toward the gates of the fort.

'I don't know how to thank you,' said Cat.

'Just stay safe, Caitriona, until I can send what help I can.'

'You know, you're really not as bad as the stories say.'

Aoife smiled and with that, Énbarr took off, speeding across the island with Cat clinging to his mane with one hand while she gripped onto the harp with the other.

The first few seconds were a terrifying blur as Énbarr sped down the hill and across the grassland, faster than should have been possible. When his hooves hit the surf, Cat almost screamed, but she need not have worried – Énbarr was indeed built for this. He galloped across the waves, cutting through the wall of mist in the space of a heartbeat.

'Hurry, Énbarr,' Cat whispered, willing him to understand. 'Take me to my granny. Take me home.'

CHAPTER NINETEEN

Taking Action

When Granny opened the front door, she took one look at the motley crew that stood before her and immediately ushered them inside and into the kitchen.

'By the look on your face, Shane Culligan, I can tell there's something very wrong. What's going on? Where is Caitriona?'

Shane launched into an explanation as the Clurichaun tried to make himself useful by boiling the kettle and setting mugs of tea in front of them, even laying a small saucer of milky tea out for Vinnie.

'Let me get this straight,' Granny said, when Shane finished his tale. 'Caitriona has been placed under a *geas* by an ancient being who has possessed the body of a witch?'

Shane nodded.

'And this *geas* involves retrieving a harp, once used by the Dagda himself to control the thoughts and feelings of others?'

Shane nodded again.

'And now Caitriona is stuck on the island of Hy-Brasil with no way of getting home again.'

'Seems like it,' said Shane.

Granny sat back and looked thoughtful. 'This is bad. I wish you'd come to me right away,' she said. 'Whatever about the *geas*, ye had to have known how dangerous it would be heading off to a mythical island on your own! Whatever were ye thinking?'

Shane burned with embarrassment. Though he had told Cat's granny the most important parts of the story, he left out the bit where they intended to use the harp themselves first before giving it to Becca … or rather to the spirit that possessed her. He figured he had landed Cat in enough trouble as it was without revealing that secret too.

'And *you*,' she said whirling around to point a finger

at the Clurichaun, who cringed under her gaze. 'You thought it would be a good idea to leave the children by themselves?'

'Well, ah, you see…' the Clurichaun stumbled over his words.

'It wasn't his fault!' said Shane, jumping to his defence. 'We sort of lied to him when we made the bargain.'

Granny gave Shane a glare that said, *Oh, don't worry, we'll deal with your lying later,* and turned back to the cowering fairy.

'I don't have time now to give you both the dressing-down you deserve,' she said. 'Not while Caitriona is trapped in this terrible bargain.' She rubbed her temples and Shane thought she looked very old and very tired. 'Shane, maybe it would be best if you head on home.'

'No! Please, I want to help.' Shane felt sick. He couldn't go home, not now, not until he knew Cat was safe again.

'All right, but at least go next door and make some kind of excuse to your uncle as to why you won't be home for dinner. The last thing we need is him mounting a search party when you don't arrive home before dark.'

Granny was right; he needed to buy himself some time

to help out. He let himself out the front door and hopped the fence into his own garden.

'Bri?' he said, noticing as soon as he stepped into the hallway that the house was eerily quiet again. He found Brian sitting at the kitchen table staring at his laptop screen with his brows furrowed in concentration.

'Brian?' Shane said again, 'Is everything OK?'

His uncle seemed startled by his appearance and Shane realised he was still in his torn and dirty school uniform and was missing both his jacket and schoolbag. Brian didn't seem to notice any of that. In fact, Shane thought, he seemed lost in his own world.

'Oh, Shaney, I didn't hear you come in,' he said. 'There's been a bit of a work emergency today. My deadline got moved and I've completely lost track of time…'

'Don't worry about it,' said Shane quickly. 'Where's Jenny and … and my mam?'

'Jenny's gone for a sleepover at her friend's and your mam's still not feeling great so she's resting in her room.'

Shane expected that, but it still hurt to hear it. A little part of him had hoped that yesterday was a fluke and she'd be back to her old self again today, but he knew from his time with the wolves that it's no use wishing things were different.

'Looks like it'll just be the two of us tonight. I'm sorry Shaney, but I don't think I'll have time to make us anything for dinner. Maybe we can get a pizza or something?'

Shane felt a rush of gratitude for his uncle. No matter what happened in future, it was nice to know that he was here looking out for them all.

'No, that's all right,' said Shane quickly. 'I'm actually going to Cat's for dinner today. I'll be home later tonight, if that's OK?'

'Yeah, fine … that works out well, actually.'

He frowned at his laptop screen again and already seemed to have forgotten Shane was there. For once, that was exactly what Shane wanted.

'Great!' said Shane, backing out of the kitchen before his uncle could ask any more questions.

He thought about changing into something a bit cleaner, but that would risk disturbing his mother, so he settled for staying in his uniform for now.

When he arrived back in Cat's house, he saw that Granny had gone into military commander mode – her default in a crisis.

'Good, you're back. We don't have long until Caitriona's mammy gets home from work, so we need to act quickly. First things first, we need to get her back from that island. Once she's safe we can start figuring out exactly what we're dealing with…'

'I think we can skip to part two of the plan,' said a quiet voice, interrupting the discussion.

Shane whipped around and found Cat standing at the kitchen door. She looked awful – her clothes were as muddy and torn as his own and tear tracks were streaked down her cheeks, but his eyes were drawn to her arms, where she was clutching a small wooden harp.

CHAPTER TWENTY

An Idea Forms

Cat placed the harp down on the floor, grateful to have the weight of it out of her arms.

'You did it,' said Shane, unable to disguise the awe in his voice. 'You actually got the harp of power.'

Before Cat could respond, Granny was on her feet. She hurried over and swept her into a tight hug. Cat could smell her perfume and it felt like home.

'I'm so glad you're safe, you've no idea how worried I've been since Shane told me what happened,' Granny said, then, pulling away, added. 'You're in a world of trouble, missy!'

'I know,' said Cat. 'And I deserve to be. I've made a

massive mistake, I know that now, and I'm sorry for dragging you into it. For dragging you all into it.' She shot the Clurichaun an apologetic glance.

'It wasn't your fault,' said Shane. 'You were under a *geas*.'

Cat turned to Shane in surprise. 'Wait, how do you know about that?'

'Vinnie told me,' he replied, as if it were the most natural thing in the world.

Vinnie bobbed his head in acknowledgement.

Well, I guess he really can talk to animals! Cat thought.

'Don't you worry, Caitriona, we'll figure out a way to break the *geas*,' said Granny.

Cat shook her head. 'You can't … it's … well, it's unbreakable. But I think there may be a way around it. It'll be dangerous, but…'

'But whatever it is, we'll face it together,' said Shane.

Granny nodded and Vinnie squeaked in agreement. Even the Clurichaun mumbled something about wanting to help however he could. Cat felt as though a massive burden had already been lifted off her shoulders. She hadn't realised how truly alone she had felt until that moment.

'How did you get off the island?' asked Shane, as Cat pulled up a chair.

'Oh dear Lord!' said Granny, who was staring out of the window in shock. 'Caitriona, why is there giant white horse in the back garden?'

'Ah, yeah, about that…'

* * *

Cat told them everything that had happened to her since Shane disappeared from the island, including meeting Aoife and learning that the *geas* could not be broken.

'Oh, Caitriona…' said Granny, and Cat was shocked to find that the older woman's eyes were filled with tears.

'But I think she gave me a way around it,' Cat said quickly, hoping to soften the blow. 'The *geas* says that I need to give the harp to Cethlenn, but it doesn't specify *when* I need to do it. So as long as I still intend on handing it over to her eventually, I'm not technically doing anything wrong.'

'Ok,' said Shane. 'I guess that makes sense … but you can't run forever, Cat.'

Vinnie began squeaking and tugging on Shane's ear.

'Ow! OK, yes, you're right,' said Shane, rubbing the stoat's head to calm him down. 'Vinnie wants to remind you that the longer we wait, the less chance Becca has.'

Cat bit her lip. She hadn't thought about that.

'I know it's not exactly the best plan, but Becca is strong. I know she can hold on just a bit longer... and I trust Aoife. I think she really will send us help as soon as she can.'

Privately, Cat wondered what Aoife could actually do, trapped as she was on the island, but she didn't want to say it out loud. Poor Vinnie was stressed enough as it was.

'What if we broke the harp?' said Shane. 'Hear me out – if the harp doesn't exist then there's nothing for you to give, so technically you wouldn't be breaking your *geas and* we would be keeping it out of Cethlenn's hands. Plus, without the harp to give her that extra power boost, we might be able to find a way to kick her out of Becca's body!'

Cat looked at the harp doubtfully. It still sat on the floor where she had left it. Though it looked like a regular wooden harp, there was a power there that hummed in the background, she knew Granny felt it too because she recognised the look of scepticism on the older woman's face.

'I suppose it's worth a try,' she said finally.

'Here, let me do it,' said the Clurichaun, jumping up from his seat, clearly keen to show how helpful he could be.

And probably also keen to break something, Cat thought.

He pulled the harp into the middle of the floor then backed up a few steps. 'Mind yerselves,' he said, 'I haven't done this before and there's a chance it might explode.'

As one, they all stood up from the table and retreated into the hallway, with Shane carrying Vinnie on his shoulder just as Becca typically would. Granny pulled the kitchen door over until there was a just a crack left for them to peek through. Cat pressed her face against it and watched as the Clurichaun cracked his knuckles and pointed at the harp.

Nothing happened.

'All right,' he mumbled to himself. 'How about a bit of this!' He reached out with both hands now and wiggled his fingers. Even from across the room, Cat could feel the power he was throwing at the harp. His face went red, and his forehead began to bead with sweat. Still the harp did not so much as twitch.

Finally, he took a deep breath and wiped his brow.

'This thing is much stronger than it looks,' he said, apologetically.

'Well, you tried,' said Granny.

'Maybe it's immune to magic?' suggested Shane. 'We could try breaking it with a hammer or something?'

The Clurichaun's eyes lit up. 'Allow me,' he said. In a flash he disappeared but before Cat could ask where he was going, he had returned wielding a giant sledgehammer.

'Where on God's green earth did you get that?' exclaimed Granny.

'The building site across town. Don't worry, I'll have it back to them before they even know it's missing.' The Clurichaun raised the sledgehammer, swaying unsteadily.

'Hold on a second!' said Granny. 'Take that outside, will ya? I'll not be having you crack a hole in Laura's floor. There'll be enough to explain if she arrives home to find a horse has eaten all her flowers.'

The Clurichaun grumbled to himself before slinging

the sledgehammer over one shoulder and grabbing the harp in his free hand. They followed him out to the back garden where Énbarr was indeed sniffing at Cat's mother's pansies with interest.

'Maybe you should send him back?' said Granny. 'I don't think Clonbridge is the best place for a magical horse.'

Cat knew Granny was right. Her mother wouldn't even let her get a kitten so she couldn't imagine she'd let her keep a stallion. She also didn't want to risk his safety. If anything happened to the horse, it would be Aoife who paid the price and Cat was sure she was already in enough trouble as it was. She tried to shoo him away, but Énbarr ignored her and moved on to nibble at the daffodils.

'Um, Shane? Maybe you could have a word with him?'

'I can try!' Shane stepped close to Énbarr and whispered a few words in his ear. Whatever he said worked – Cat could swear the horse bowed to Shane before leaping over the hedge in one swift movement and galloping away. Shane looked unbearably smug, and she wondered if this new-found power of his was going to turn out to be extremely annoying for her.

Once the coast was clear, Cat, Granny and Shane stood

well back from the Clurichaun so he could make his second attempt at breaking the harp.

He set the harp down in the grass, then he reached the sledgehammer back as far as it would go and swung with all his might. The hammer was centimetres from the harp when it seemed to hit an invisible barrier, the force of which caused the Clurichaun to yelp in pain.

He was still hopping from foot to foot cursing to himself when Granny said, 'Well, that settles it. The harp can't be destroyed,'

'Which means I have no choice. I need to give Cethlenn the harp eventually or…'

'Or nothing,' said Granny sharply. 'There's no other option. You'll give over the harp, and we'll deal with what comes next.'

For a while, they all stood silent, contemplating what that might look like. What did Cethlenn plan to do once she had the harp? Cat knew from her story that she considered this land to be unfairly taken from her… Would she try and claim it back? Cat shuddered. There had to be another way out of this.

All of a sudden, Vinnie began squeaking wildly.

'Hold on,' said Shane, 'You're speaking too fast... I can't...'

'He's saying that he has an idea,' said the Clurichaun.

Shane nodded. 'He says that ... that Cethlenn's hold on Becca isn't complete yet. Maybe, if we could distract Cethlenn for long enough, Becca could find a way to cast Cethlenn out before she actually uses the harp.'

'OK,' Cat said slowly, trying to sort the plan through in her mind as she spoke. 'So I give Cethlenn – in Becca's body – the harp, then we cause a commotion, something that gives Becca enough time to regain control of her body and cast her out...'

'Would that break the *geas*?' asked Granny, turning to the Clurichaun, who chewed his lip thoughtfully at the question.

'Well ... yes,' said slowly, 'As long as you hand it over before the witch takes back control of her body, it would count. But I won't lie to ye, it's a risky move. The Fomorians were mighty beings back in the day, and you can be sure that Cethlenn's power will be growing by the hour. I'm sorry, but I'm not sure this witch has enough power to get the job done. There's no being on Earth who can stand against the Fomorians.'

'What other choice do we have?' asked Shane.

Everyone fell silent, lost in their own thoughts. Cat's eyes fell on the harp. Such a small thing to be causing so much trouble. If only the Tuatha Dé Danann had taken it to the Otherworld when they left then none of this would be happening. It wasn't fair. They should be the ones cleaning up this mess.

'Wait!' she cried as an idea began to take shape in her mind. 'I know what we have to do! It's risky, but I think it could work.'

* * *

'I don't like this Caitriona,' said Granny when Cat finished outlining her plan. 'It's too dangerous and too much could go wrong.'

'What choice do we have?' said Cat. 'We can't risk Cethlenn using the harp. I only wish … I wish that Aoife had been able to send help in time.'

'I think we may be of some assistance there.'

Cat's heart did a somersault. She knew that voice. She

turned to find Conn standing at the garden gate in his human form, with two wolves at his side – Sorcha and Domhnall. Cat would have hugged them if she didn't think Sorcha would literally bite her hand off.

'Good Lord,' said Granny, 'This place is turning into a zoo! Quick, everyone get inside before the neighbours spot you.'

The kitchen was crowded, even with Domhnall and Sorcha back in their human forms. They looked around them warily, taking in all the modern conveniences. How long had it been since they had been out in the world? Centuries? It must be hard for them, Cat thought. She learned there were four other wolves waiting for them just outside Clonbridge. She hoped they were well hidden because she dreaded to think what would happen if some local out for a country ramble stumbled on a pack of supposedly extinct predators.

'What are you doing here?' asked Cat.

'We came to repay our debt,' responded Conn. 'Shortly after you left our village, we received … a visitor.' Conn could not hide the disgust in his voice and Cat knew then that Aoife must have appeared to them in her demon form. 'The guardian of the fort told us what had transpired. She told us to hurry to this place and to help you however we can. Our warriors are at your disposal.'

Aoife had done it. She promised Cat help and she had come through. For the first time all day, Cat began to feel hopeful. It would be difficult, and the battle was far from over, but at least they finally stood a chance.

CHAPTER TWENTY-ONE

The Plan is Set in Motion

Things began to move quickly. It was decided that, with Cethlenn most likely growing stronger, there was no time to waste. If they were going to act, it must be now.

Granny called Cat's mother and explained that Cat was going to come and stay with her tonight.

'She just needs … a bit of time,' Granny said, in a low voice, trying unsuccessfully to keep Cat from hearing. She could guess what her mother had just asked, though. *Is she still mad at me?*

Cat swallowed and asked Granny if she could have the

phone.

'Hi, Mam,' she said, once Granny handed it over.

'Hi, Kitty-Cat,' her mother replied in that false-bright voice Cat had come to know too well these past few days. 'Granny was saying you want to stay at her house tonight. Are you sure? I'm just after getting Mikey from the child-minder and I was thinking I could swing by the chipper and grab us a takeaway and then maybe we could watch a film or something?'

'Maybe tomorrow,' Cat said. 'Me and Granny have already made plans.'

Cat could almost feel her mother's disappointment down the phone.

'I'm sorry,' Cat said quickly and was surprised to find her eyes had filled with tears. 'I'm sorry for how I've acted this week… I know I've been—'

'It's OK,' her mother said, interrupting her. 'I under-stand. I didn't handle things the best and…' She took a deep breath. 'And I'm sorry too. I really am. I love you, Cat.'

'I love you too, Mam. I'll see you tomorrow.'

Cat wiped her eyes and handed the phone back to

Granny who mumbled her own goodbyes.

'We better hurry,' Granny said, after she hung up. 'If Laura's at the childminder's that means we have fifteen minutes at best to get out of here.'

'OK, then we need to pick a place to lure Cethlenn to,' said Cat. 'It should probably be somewhere away from town in case it all goes wrong.'

Vinnie began squeaking.

'He said he knows a place,' said Shane, translating for the stoat. 'There's a holy well he and Becca were investigating last week that reeked of old magic. He thinks that's where Cethlenn found them.'

Conn nodded. He had been standing silently as they made their arrangements, but now he spoke up. 'Wells are conduits between this world and the Otherworld. It would make sense that the Fomorian was drawn to it.'

That was welcome news to Cat. It would make the next part of her plan easier.

'Can you tell us how to get there?' Cat asked Vinnie, who bobbed his head up and down.

'He said he can show me on a map,' said Shane.

With that settled, the only remaining part of the plan

was to figure out how to get Cethlenn to the field.

'Can we send the Clurichaun?' asked Shane.

Granny shook her head. 'No. He's a fairy, which means he can't tell a lie. If she asks him why you didn't bring the harp straight to her the whole plan will be out the window.'

'What about you?' asked Cat. She had been hoping to find a way to keep Granny safe and this might be the perfect opportunity.

In answer, Granny pursed her lips and crossed her arms. 'Oh no,' she said. 'You'll not be getting rid of me that easily Caitriona Anne Donnelly. I'd never forgive myself if something happened to you.'

'Vinnie can go,' cut in Shane before things between Cat and her Granny descended into a full-blown argument. 'He can see Becca's spirit so he can warn her about the plan and make sure she's ready to take her body back when the time comes.'

Cat wasn't sure, but it seemed like it might be their only option, so she agreed.

'All right,' she said looking around her at the rag-tag group of companions. There was nothing left to do but act. 'Let's go.'

The wolves ran on ahead to scout out the area and Vinnie scurried away, promising to wait long enough to ensure they had time to get to the well. The humans considered having the Clurichaun transport them there by fairy road again, but with three of them plus the harp in tow, he wasn't sure he could manage.

'It's probably for the best anyway,' said Cat, who remembered how dizzy it had made her feel. She needed to keep her wits about her if she had any chance against Cethlenn. It was eventually decided that Granny would drive them there in the ancient blue Nissan Micra that she normally only used for getting her weekly shopping. She had been using it more often since her heart attack when the doctors had told her to take it easy. Unfortunately, her growing familiarity with the car hadn't made her a better driver and Cat was nervous as she slid into the back seat beside Shane. She whispered to him to buckle up as Granny started the car and pulled away from the house as though she were driving a Formula One race car.

'Woah!' said Shane, his eyes wide.

'I know,' Cat whispered back. 'Granny doesn't believe

in doing anything by half.'

As they passed Becca's house, Cat found herself holding her breath. She was sure Cethlenn would feel the harp's presence and chase them down the street. She clung to it and willed it not to project its magic so much. It must have worked or maybe they just got lucky, but they managed to pass by unnoticed. When Granny turned out of the estate and onto Main Street, Cat allowed herself to relax just a bit. The danger wasn't past – far from it – but they had completed the first hurdle.

She tried to settle back and relax, but for the entirety of the short journey, Cat looked out the window and imagined all the various ways her plan could go wrong – maybe Cethlenn would catch Vinnie before he could warn Becca? Maybe she would be waiting for them at the well? Maybe they wouldn't be able to distract her before she used the harp? Around and around the worries swirled in her mind until, all too soon, Granny was pulling over into the car park of an old church Vinnie had told them about.

The wolves were already waiting for them in their animal form. Cat found it strange to see them just milling around a car park; she was glad the church was a little out of the way. She didn't want to imagine what would happen if anyone else saw them!

The wolf Cat recognised as Sorcha inclined her head as if to say, 'Follow me.'

The sun had already set by the time they climbed the fence and made their way across an overgrown field. When they were further away from the road, Sorcha shifted back into her human shape.

'The well is over there,' she said, pointing to a tangled clump of brambles at the far edge of the field.

'That's it?' said Cat in surprise. She had been expecting something more imposing. Something made of stone that you could lower a bucket into like the wells she had seen in storybooks. This was like any other forgotten patch of the Irish countryside, with nothing to indicate that anything special lay there other than the faint tang of magic she could sense on the air.

'There are thousands of holy wells all over the country,' said Granny. 'Many are still in decent condition but there are plenty that are more like this – overgrown and forgotten by all save a few locals.'

'This one feels very old,' said Cat, although she wasn't sure how she knew.

'Oh, that it is, girl,' confirmed the Clurichaun. 'Holy wells have long been sites of pilgrimage, even before the coming of Christianity. There were probably people coming to this place in search of healing for thousands of years.'

Seems as good a place as any to face an ancient warrior queen, Cat thought.

'Come,' Sorcha said to Granny and the Clurichaun. 'It's almost time.'

Granny gave Cat an unreadable look. They had argued about this back in the house. She had wanted to stand by her granddaughter's side and face whatever was coming together, but Cat managed to convince her that if she was there, Cethlenn would be suspicious. It was bad enough that Shane would be with her, but at least Cethlenn had seen him before and heard the story of their Halloween trials. She would hopefully presume that Shane had just come along for the adventure. Granny eventually agreed to wait with the wolves, hidden among the trees in the small grove that flanked the field, close enough that she could keep an eye on things.

'At the first sign of trouble, you yell for me, and I'll come running,' she said.

Cat agreed although she didn't know what good an almost seventy-year-old woman with a slightly dodgy hip would do in a fight against Cethlenn.

When Granny turned to follow Sorcha into the line of trees, Cat grabbed the Clurichaun and whispered to him, 'If this goes badly I want you to get Granny out of here, OK? Take the fairy road if you have to.'

The Clurichaun nodded and Cat was satisfied that she had done as much as she could.

Finally, she and Shane were left alone.

'You can go too,' she said to him. 'You don't need to be here when Cethlenn arrives.'

Shane shook his head. 'We started this together and we'll end it together.'

'What if it goes badly?' she asked, her voice shaking slightly.

'It won't,' he said, and he sounded so confident, Cat almost believed him.

The darkness had truly descended by now and the

night had grown cold enough for Cat to be able see her breath fog out in front of her. She shivered and pretended to herself it was because of the cold.

'Shane,' she said, 'I'm sorry for … well, for everything.'

'We've been over this,' he said. 'You don't have to apologise; you were under a *geas*!'

'I don't think I can use that as an excuse. Not entirely. Cethlenn may have set me on the path but, deep down, I think a little part of me really did want to use the harp to make my mam forget all about Darren. When she told me the other day, I was just so hurt. I wanted to make that pain go away. I was selfish and mean and when you tried to help me see that, I was horrible to you too.'

'All right, maybe you were a little mean and selfish,' said Shane. 'But so was I. Things have been so good lately with my mam, you know?'

Cat nodded. She did know. Shane had been like a whole new person since his uncle Brian moved in. He was lighter and happier, like his old self once again.

'When she took a turn the other day, it was awful. It felt like we were going backwards, and I swore I would do whatever it took to stop that from happening again,' he continued. 'When you told me about the harp, it seemed perfect, like it was the answer to all my prayers. If you were being selfish, then so was I.'

'At least you realised it first.'

Shane smiled. 'I did. Which means I win the "stop being selfish competition." You can give me my prize later.'

Cat shoved him slightly and rolled her eyes, but she was glad to know that he had forgiven her and that he was by her side for what would come next.

She looked to the sky as the first stars began to appear. It wouldn't be long now.

CHAPTER TWENTY-TWO

The Call of the Harp

ethlenn was restless. It had been two days since she had placed the *geas* on the girl and still there was no sign of the harp. Had she been wrong to think the child worthy enough to retrieve it for her? She pulled at her hair, well, the *witch's* ridiculous pink hair, and let out a roar of frustration. Hundreds of years she had waited for her vengeance and now it was so close she could almost taste it. Where *was* the girl?

At least there had been no sign of the witch for a while. After a few more futile attempts to push Cethlenn's spirit out of her body, she seemed to have finally given up. She wasn't gone, not yet. Cethlenn could still sense her essence somewhere close by. But she knew it wouldn't be long before she disappeared for good. Then this body would be Cethlenn's forever… or until she found something better at least.

She moved through the witch's house, searching for something to occupy her mind when she heard it: a faint thump coming from upstairs. She knew right away what it was – the stoat had returned. She had smelled the creature the previous morning when she returned to the bedroom and knew that it must have squeezed its way through the crack in the open window. The bond between a witch and a familiar was strong and Cethlenn had suspected it would return again. This time she was determined to catch it and rid herself of that annoyance once and for all. She smiled to herself. At least this would provide the distraction she needed.

She scaled the stairs as quietly as she could and crept toward the open bedroom door. There it was – the little rat was bobbing up and down speaking to the witch's spirit, which was even fainter now, Cethlenn noted with pleasure.

In a single leap, she burst into the room and lunged for

the stoat. The creature writhed and twisted in her grip, but still she held firm.

'Let him go!' said the witch, but her voice sounded distant. Cethlenn ignored her and squeezed the stoat harder, causing the creature to yelp.

'Now, let's get rid of you once and for all.'

'Wait!' squeaked the stoat. 'If you kill me, you'll never learn about the harp!'

'What do you mean?' she snapped.

'I know where it is!' he said.

She loosened her grip slightly, making sure the stoat could not wriggle away and he told her everything. As he told his tale, she could feel the red mist of battle descending over her. So the girl had the harp and had not brought it straight to her? Foolish child. She would pay for that. Cethlenn dropped the stoat, no longer concerned with the creature. She had one goal now and one goal only – to get the harp. Though she had waited for this moment for many long years, she could not stand to wait even a second more. She needed to get to the well.

She could feel the witch's muscles screaming in protest as she dragged her body out the door and into the rapidly darkening night and began to run. She did her best to ignore the pain in her calves and the tightness in her chest and imagined instead that she was back in her own body, her true body. The body of a warrior. A Fomorian queen who could run from dawn until dusk without ever finding herself out of breath. As she pushed on, she could feel the harp at the edge of her awareness, drawing her toward it like a beacon. Soon it would be hers.

Cat's Song

They had been in the field for around twenty minutes when Cat felt it. The pulsing rage coming toward her.

'She's here,' Cat whispered and felt Shane snap to attention by her side. 'Get ready.'

Cat straightened and gripped the harp tightly just as a figure appeared before her. Cethlenn. Even in the early evening gloom, Cat could see she was entirely transformed. Although she still had Becca's features, her kind face was twisted in rage and power radiated out of her in waves. There was no sign of Becca – the *real* Becca. Had Vinnie gotten to her in time? Had he told her the full plan before Cethlenn caught him? She had no way of knowing, but she had to hope that Becca's spirit would arrive soon or the whole plan would fall apart.

Cethlenn was moving toward Cat quickly, too quickly, as though her body was propelled by some otherworldly force. In seconds, she was just feet away. Her eyes raked over the harp and Cat could sense her hunger.

'Becca,' said Cat, praying her voice didn't shake. 'What are you doing here?'

'I might ask the same of you,' said Cethlenn. Her voice was different now. It was deeper than Becca's and harsher. 'I see you have retrieved the harp. Why did you not bring it to me directly?'

Cat smiled at Becca and pretended to be confused.

'But did you not tell me the other day that I could use the harp myself?'

'I said no such thing!'

'Are you sure? Because I seem to remember you telling me that you knew about something that could solve all my problems. Are you telling me that you were never going to let me use it? That hardly seems fair, considering the trouble I went to get the harp for you.'

Cethlenn curled a lip and Cat could almost hear the snarl she held back. 'Yes, yes, of course I intended to let you use the harp. But later. Now, give it to me.' She reached forward, her hands grasping for the harp.

'I think you're lying to me, Becca … Or should I say Cethlenn?'

Of all the reactions Cat thought Cethlenn might have, tipping her head back and letting out a booming laugh wasn't one of them. Cat looked to Shane and saw the same surprised look on his face.

'So, you figured it out, did you, girl? Who told you? Was it the fool who guards the treasures of the Tuatha Dé Danann? No matter. Already my power grows stronger by the minute and once I have the harp, I will be unstoppable. I can make your life very difficult, girl, or very easy. It all depends on how much you try my patience.'

Still Cat kept hold of the harp, biding as much time as she could, hoping that Becca's spirit wasn't far away.

'Foolish child,' she hissed. 'If you know who I am then you also know about the *geas* I've placed you under. You cannot keep the harp from me and expect to live.'

Cat finally noticed a silvery wisp hovering in the

air, coming ever closer to Cethlenn. Was it Becca? She couldn't tell.

'Cat, you'd better give it to her,' urged Shane.

'Listen to your friend,' said Cethlenn.

Cat bit her lip. Her time had run out. She took a deep breath and stared Cethlenn in the eye.

'You want the harp?' she said. 'Then take it!'

The harp was heavy, but Cat flung it from her with all the strength she could muster. The second she threw the harp toward Cethlenn, she felt something inside her snap. The voice in her head that had been urging her forward all day was finally completely gone. The *geas* was broken – she was free. But she had no time to celebrate. As Cethlenn lunged for the harp, Cat yelled at the top of her voice, 'Now!'

From out of the trees streamed seven wolves. Shane grabbed Cat and pulled her back as the pack descended on Cethlenn.

Cethlenn was so intent on grabbing the harp that she didn't notice the wolves until they were almost upon her. She opened her mouth to scream just as the lead wolf – Conn, Cat thought – clamped his teeth around her wrist.

Her howl was enough to shake the bones of the earth, but still she didn't drop the harp. Two more wolves were on her now, snarling and snapping at her. Cat had warned them to take care with Becca's body, but she didn't know how much control they retained in their wolf forms. She had to hope Cethlenn would drop the harp before they did too much damage.

'Hurry, Cat,' Shane hissed, dragging her across the field toward the clump of brambles that hid the holy well. They needed to put as much distance between themselves and Cethlenn as possible if they were to have any hope of the plan working.

As Cat whipped around, she saw that Cethlenn was fully surrounded, swiping at the wolves with the harp, trying to push them back enough to play it. One of the wolves behind her lunged for her hamstring with teeth bared. Cethlenn looked over her shoulder in shock – and it was enough. In the split second she was distracted, Domhnall morphed back into his human form and ripped the harp from her hands.

Cathlenn screamed, making to charge after him, but the wolves managed to hold her at bay. Domhnall began running, holding the heavy harp under one arm as if it weighed nothing. He sprinted toward Cat and Shane and threw the harp at their feet before immediately changing back into his wolf form and plunging back into battle.

Cat picked up the harp and took a breath.

'Do you know what you're doing?' asked Shane.

'Not a clue,' Cat said. 'But I have to try.'

Back in Granny's kitchen, when they discussed the epic scale of the problem they were facing, an idea came to Cat like a bolt out of the blue. They had the wolves to provide a distraction and hopefully they had Becca ready to seize control of her body again, but that would still leave them with the furious spirit of a Fomorian queen to deal with and Cat was sure that, whether she had a body or not, she was too powerful for her to take on. That's why she wasn't going to. She was going to summon someone else who could.

'Hurry,' said Shane, turning to keep an eye on the battle as Cat settled herself behind the harp and began to play. As her finger plucked the first string, a bright, clear sound rang out over the field. When she reached the second string, she began to chant. The words didn't rhyme, and

Cat was certainly no great singer, but she poured all her hopes and worries into the song and sent it out in the world, hoping to reach the Dagda himself.

'Come back, warriors of the Tuatha Dé Danann, come back. Return to the land you left long ago. Come back and defend this land. Come back and *fight*.'

She plucked the strings faster and even though she could barely play the tin whistle, let alone a harp, it didn't seem to matter. Once she started, it was as though the music composed itself under her fingertips.

'Nothing's happening!' said Shane, so Cat began to chant louder and hoped that wherever he was, the Dagda could hear it.

'Come back, come back. Please! Come back and fight!'

She heard a cry from behind her. It was Shane, yelling at her.

'Watch out! Cethlenn's free and she's coming this way!'

Cat opened her eyes, expecting to see Becca's body rushing across the field. Instead she just had time to make out the faint silvery figure that hurtled toward her before a force slammed into her mind and everything went dark.

CHAPTER TWENTY-FOUR

A Great Power Rises

Invisible claws raked at Cat's mind. It was Cethlenn; she clearly couldn't escape the wolves, so in a desperate attempt to reach the harp she had decided to leave Becca's body behind and take over Cat's instead.

Give me control, girl, said Cethlenn, her voice twisted and cruel.

Cat fought against her, pushing her back as hard as she could. Somewhere in the distance she thought she could hear Shane yelling at her.

'Fight her, Cat! You have to keep playing!'

The harp. Her attention was focused on keeping Cethlenn out of her mind that she had stopped playing. She didn't know if she would be able to concentrate enough to play and keep the Fomorian at bay, but she had to try. It was her only chance. She forced her arms to move, forced herself to pick up the harp.

Useless girl, why bother to fight me? It's much easier to give in.

Cat felt those invisible claws peeling back her defences. Soon they would be wide open and then nothing would stop Cethlenn from casting Cat's spirit out of her own body.

Let me have control and I'll do what you asked – I'll play the song that returns your mother to you. Just give in.

'No!' Cat screamed the word into the night. With a huge effort she plucked at the harp strings and took up her chant again. 'Hear me, Dagda. Hear me, warriors of the Tuatha Dé Danann. Come back and fight!'

Suddenly, the whole world went bright. Cat shaded her eyes against it. She felt Cethlenn's attack grow slack as her spirit let out a howl of defiance. The light died down and when Cat opened her eyes again, there stood before her a host of shining warriors. There were so many of them – men and women, young and old, and all of them were beauty and light. Cat found herself staring with her mouth open as a tall, broad man with a large bushy beard of bright red stepped forward and held out his hand to her.

'I believe you have something of mine, child.' It was the Dagda himself.

Unable to speak, Cat handed over the harp and the Dagda smiled at her and began to play. His playing was nothing like Cat's. It was beautiful and haunting and although she didn't understand the words he spoke she could feel the Dagda's command woven into the notes of the song. *Show yourself*, it said.

Suddenly, the silvery shadow that had been attacking her turned and began to flee. Cat worried that Cethlenn was going to escape, but the Dagda seemed unconcerned and continued to play his song. The shadow was halfway across the field when it began to grow more solid. First, her legs appeared, then her torso and arms and finally, her head. Cethlenn, finally revealed in her true form. With a snarl, she whipped around to face them, and Cat could see that she was tall and broad of shoulder with corded muscles in her arms. A warrior's build. Her hair was dark and pulled back in a messy plait that fell down her back. Her face was scarred from the many battles she had fought over the years and her eyes were filled with deep, venomous hatred for the enemies that stood before her.

The Dagda continued to play, and Cat watched in awe as one of the Tuatha Dé Danann, a young man whose face shone bright as the sun, stepped forward, spear in hand. *This must be Lugh,* Cat realised. Cethlenn's own grandson – the one who had killed her husband Balor on the fields of Moytura so long ago. To her credit, Cethlenn did not blink or try to escape as he struck her with the spear. She opened her mouth to yell one final curse at the Tuatha Dé Danann, but whatever it was, it was whipped away by a roaring wind that swirled around her. It swirled faster and faster, picking up leaves and twigs as it went. It was as though Cethlenn was trapped in the centre of a tiny tornado. Just as the wind seemed to reach a fever pitch, the Dagda played a final note on his harp and then it was gone, taking Cethlenn with it.

'What did you do to her?' asked Shane, who had stayed by Cat's side the entire time.

'We sent her to the Otherworld, where she should have

gone a long time ago,' said the Dagda. 'This world is no place for her kind any more, just as it is no place for ours. It is long past time we all moved on.'

He smiled down at Cat who realised she was still in the mud. He extended a hand to pull her up and his touch felt like electricity. His magic was so strong, it was like nothing she had ever felt before.

A great power will rise. What if the wolves' prophecy had not been about Cethlenn, but about this? About the return of the Tuatha Dé Danann.

'If Cethlenn had got her hands on this harp, the repercussions would have been disastrous. You have done a great deed today by helping us put a stop to her once and for all. Tell me, child, what is your name?' said the Dagda.

'Caitriona, but my friends call me Cat.'

'Well then, Cat, I believe we owe you a debt. Name your price and if it is within my power it shall be done.'

Cat felt herself reeling. She was being offered a gift from a god. What would she ask for? The Dagda had put no limitations on it, only that it be within his power to grant. Ultimately, there was only one thing she really wanted right then.

'Don't punish Aoife,' she said. 'Please. I know she was meant to keep the harp safe but—'

The Dagda raised his hand and Cat stopped speaking. 'Do not worry, Cat. Aoife will not be punished. She has served us well for many years and is welcome to join us in the Otherworld as soon as she likes.'

'Well, in that case…'

A shout from across the field grabbed her attention. It was Domhnall and he was waving at them.

Cat and Shane raced over and found Granny and Conn bent over Becca's unconscious form, trying to get her to wake up.

'What happened?' said Cat, 'Is she alive?'

'She is,' replied Granny, 'Just about.'

'When Cethlenn left her body, we saw the spirit of the witch enter into it,' said Conn.

'Then why isn't she awake?'

'I'm afraid we may have injured her too badly in the fight. I'm sorry. We tried our best to be gentle, but Cethlenn fought us so hard…'

'It's not your fault,' said Shane. 'You did what you had to.'

Cat looked around for the Dagda and found him standing close by, his face grave.

'Help her,' Cat pleaded. 'Please, heal Becca. That's what I want in return.'

'The witch is gravely ill. I do not think I will be able to heal her,' said the Dagda and Cat felt her heart sink. 'But my daughter Brigid can.'

From the midst of the Tuatha Dé Danann, a beautiful young woman stepped forward and Cat thought the air suddenly smelled of spring.

'I would be glad to help your friend,' she said.

She sat down at Becca's side and took one of her hands gently in her own. She closed her eyes and whispered a few words that Cat could not understand.

With a gasp, Becca sat up and looked around her with confusion.

'Who are…? What just…? How did I…?'

'Rest now,' said Brigid. 'You are healed, but you are still weak.'

'Oh my goodness!' said Granny staring down at Brigid with shining eyes. 'Is it really you?'

Brigid smiled at Granny. 'It is indeed. And it is a pleasure to meet a fellow Wise Woman. I am glad to see that the old ways have not entirely been forgotten.' With that, she returned to stand at her father's side and left Granny completely dumbfounded.

'Now, there is one more we must attend to before we return to the Otherworld,' said the Dagda. 'Conn of the wolf clan. For the great deeds you have performed this day, I invite you and your family to join us in the Otherworld where there are plenty of deer to hunt and fish to catch and where the pastures never grow empty.'

Conn bowed his head. 'We gratefully accept.'

'Then it is time for us to take our leave of this world once again. Take care of it for us, won't you?'

Before Cat could respond to say that yes, of course she would, the Tuatha Dé Danann, along with the wolf clan, disappeared and she found herself alone in the field with Shane, Granny and Becca.

'Is it safe to come out?' said the Clurichaun from his hiding place in the trees.

'Yes, you big ninny!' said Granny. 'You can come out; the fight is over, and we won.'

'I'm sorry, but what just happened?' asked a clearly still

dazed Becca.

'Long story,' said Cat, 'We'll fill you in later.'

'Where's Vinnie?' asked Shane, the worry in his voice evident.

'He's fine. Once he told Cethlenn where the harp was, she dropped him like a hot coal. I just had time to make sure he wasn't hurt before I took off after her.'

Shane sighed with relief.

'I still can't believe what just happened,' Becca continued. 'I mean, I thought the Tuatha Dé Danann and all that were just myths. I never expected to meet them in person, let alone be possessed by a Fomorian! Come to think of it, I never thought I would be possessed by *any-thing*. I guess I still have a lot to learn. You know, for once in my life, I'm completely and totally speechless. Well, no, actually there was that one time…'

Granny turned to Cat. 'Talks a lot that one, doesn't she?'

'You get used to it,' said Cat.

'Come on,' said Granny, pulling Cat in close for a hug. 'Let's go home.'

CHAPTER TWENTY-FIVE

New Beginnings

If Cat thought that the events of the past few hours would be enough to allow her to escape one of Granny's lectures, she was sorely mistaken. After they dropped off Becca and Shane, they went back to Granny's house and Cat had to deal with Granny giving out to her the whole way. By the time they pulled back into Granny's driveway she seemed to have gotten it out of her system.

'I was so worried about you, Caitriona,' she said, and Cat could hear the sadness in her voice. 'And I'm sorry I wasn't able to protect you.'

'I was under a *geas*, remember?' said Cat 'I don't think there's anything you could have done.'

Granny nodded. 'Oh, don't think I forget that! Once that Becca one has a bit of time to recover I'll be marching you straight over there and giving you both a good talking-to about being more careful around magic. I mean honestly, she calls herself a witch! There's a lot I have to teach you both so you can protect yourselves better in future. But...' Granny paused. 'I suppose it might be good for her to teach you a few things too. Her magic is very different to mine and since you seem determined to constantly get yourself in trouble, it wouldn't do you any harm to have a few more tricks up your sleeve.'

Cat beamed. She was going to learn magic!

The next morning, Cat woke bright and early and told Granny she wanted to go home because there was something she needed to do. She raced home and found her mother in the kitchen, mashing a banana and some Weetabix for Mikey.

'Cat! You're home early.'

Cat didn't say anything, but went straight to her mother and hugged her tight. She didn't say anything else; she didn't need to. They stayed that way for a full minute before Mikey started crying because he wanted a hug too.

'What do you want to do today?' asked her mother after she planted a kiss on top of Cat's head. 'We can do anything you like!'

Cat took a deep breath. 'I was thinking that maybe I could meet Darren.'

'Are you sure?' her mother asked. 'You don't have to. Not yet. We can give it time.'

'No, I'm sure,' said Cat, 'I really want to meet him.' The smile her mother gave her was enough to know that she was doing the right thing.

Her mother sent a few text messages and let Cat know that Darren would be coming over for lunch and that he was bringing home-made Victoria sponge for them to have after.

Cat said that sounded great, and then excused herself to go to her room. She felt her stomach twist with nerves and tried to distract herself by writing the events of the past few days in the Book of Secrets while it was all still fresh in her mind. It almost worked because, when the doorbell rang at one o'clock she almost jumped out of her chair.

She was halfway down the stairs when her mother

opened the door to reveal Shane, who grinned at her.

'Hiya, Shaney!' said her mother. 'Do you want to come in?'

'No, thank you,' replied Shane. 'I'm just calling to see if Cat wants to go to the cinema with us. Brian is bringing me, my mam and Jenny to see the newest Disney film. I wanted to go and see that film with the space battle, but they all voted against me.'

'You can go if you want, Cat. It's all right, honestly,' said her mother and Cat knew she meant it.

'No thanks,' she said to Shane. 'Maybe next time. Today ... today I have plans.'

Her mother smiled and hurried back into the kitchen when the fire alarm went off.

'She's making soup,' said Cat shaking her head. 'How do you burn soup?'

'You're too used to the Clurichaun's fancy creations these days,' said Shane. 'Are you OK, Cat? You look a bit nervous or something.'

Cat nodded. 'I'm fine. I'm ... I'm meeting my mam's boyfriend soon.'

Shane's eyes widened. 'Oh, well. Good luck!'

There was a beep from the road and Shane looked over his shoulder to find Brian waving out the window of his car. 'Come on, slowpokes! We'll be late and I like watching the trailers.'

'All right, hold your horses, Bri, we're coming,' said another voice. One Cat hadn't heard in a very long time. It was Shane's mother, locking the front door behind her and taking Jenny by the hand.

As if reading her thoughts, Shane turned to Cat, 'She has good days and bad, but if there's something I learned from Conn and the wolves, it's that we should enjoy the good ones as much as we can and just take it one day at a time.'

Brian beeped again and Shane took off, calling his goodbyes to Cat.

Cat was about to close the door when another car pulled up in front of the house. One she had never seen before. A man with slightly messy brown hair and thick, black-framed glasses got out of the driver's seat and reached back in and took out a plastic box with a very squished-looking cake shoved inside. *This must be Darren,* Cat thought. She realised he looked just as nervous as she felt.

Before she could say anything, her mother was at her side and the smile on her face was bright enough to light up the whole street. She took the cake from Darren with plenty of 'oohs and ahhs' at how delicious it looked (it didn't) and then she made her introductions.

'Cat this is Darren, and Darren this is my brilliant daughter, Cat.'

'It's nice to meet you, I've heard loads about you,' he said.

'What are we doing all standing in the doorway like this?' said her mother. 'Come on in, I've made us some soup and sandwiches for lunch.'

As Darren and her mother headed for the kitchen, Cat hung back for a second to make sure she was ready for what came next. She took a deep breath.

One day at a time, she thought, and closed the door behind her.

Finding Home

On an island surrounded by mist, in a place out of time, a woman sat alone in a stone fortress and looked out over the ocean.

The call was faint at first. So faint she might have missed it if she had not been waiting for it for hundreds of years.

'Aoife…'

She knew that voice, or thought she did. It had been so long since she heard it that she could have been wrong. She did not allow herself to hope but she did arise and follow the sound of the voice. It led her out of the great hall, through the courtyard and out of the fortress itself.

'Aoife,' it said again. It called her down the mountainside, past the abandoned wolf village, and toward the rocky shore where the island met the sea. She found Énbarr waiting for her on the beach, stomping his feet impatiently on the sand.

'Aoife,' the voice was clear now and Aoife felt tears stream down her face. She knew for sure who it was now. It was the voice of Fionnuala, the daughter of Lir, the child she had wronged so long ago.

'Your penance is paid,' said Fionnuala. 'You are forgiven and now it is time to come home.'

Aoife mounted Énbarr. She didn't look back as the horse sped across the waves. He carried her, not toward Ireland, but toward another place, a place she thought she would never be welcome. As the light of the Otherworld shone upon her face, Aoife sent up a silent 'thank you' to the girl who had helped her find her way home.

From Caitriona Donnelly's Book of Secrets

AOIFE: According to legend, Aoife was the second wife of a man called Lir and stepmother to his children. She got jealous of how much Lir loved his children and used her magic powers to turn them into swans. For doing that, Aoife was cursed to live out her days as a demon of the air. She's actually pretty nice though!

BRIGID: St Brigid was a woman who lived in Ireland hundreds of years ago and performed many miracles. She may or may not be the same person as Brigid, the goddess of spring and fertility (among other things) who was a member of the Tuatha Dé Danann (see entry on TUATHA DÉ DANANN for more). It's complicated!

CETHLENN: The queen of the Fomorians (see entry on **FOMORIANS** below). She spent hundreds of years living as a ghost in a holy well before she decided to possess my friend Becca and put a *geas* on me (see *GEAS* for more info). Unlike Aoife, she really *was* a villain!

THE DAGDA: The Chieftain of the Tuatha Dé Danann (see below for more on the **TUATHA DÉ DANANN**). He was the god of weather, agriculture and fertility and he owned three magic treasures, including *Uaithne*, the harp of power (see below). He's also the father of Brigid.

DRUIDS: Druids were kind of like the priests of ancient Ireland, but they didn't wear all black like the priests today do. They had special powers in healing and would often use small stones with markings on them called 'runes' to tell the future. Ferdia of the wolf clan is a druid and that's how he knew of the prophecy involving Cethlenn and the Harp of Power.

ÉNBARR: A magical horse owned by Manannán Mac Lir, who was god of the sea (no relation to Lir, husband of Aoife). Énbarr can ride over waves with supernatural speed. He also likes eating flowers from my mam's garden.

FAMILIARS: Animals that have special bonds with witches. Some witches can talk with their familiars – like Becca and

Vinnie – and some can't, but they all have a deep connection that helps when it comes to casting spells.

FOMORIANS: An ancient warrior tribe that lived in Ireland thousands of years ago. Some people claim the Fomorians were ugly, gigantic monsters, but they were just really unfriendly. Their leaders were a man known as Balor of the Evil Eye and his wife, Cethlenn. Their enemies were the Tuatha Dé Danann and they spent years fighting with them until they were eventually defeated once and for all at the Battle of Moytura.

GEAS: A magical obligation a bit like a curse. When a *geas* is placed on you it means you *have to* do whatever is commanded of you or else you die. A *geas* is unbreakable, but there are ways around them, if you're clever about it!

HOLY WELL: There are lots of holy wells all over the country. Before Christianity came to Ireland, these were important sites for pagans, who believed that wells were a gateway to the Otherworld. These days, most holy wells are associated with a saint and are said to have healing water (but I think I'll stick to drinking water from the tap, thanks).

HY-BRASIL: A magical island that's hidden from view by a thick wall of fog. It was one of the strongholds of the Tuatha Dé Danann. When they left for the Otherworld, they gave the island over to a tribe of shapeshifting wolves and made Aoife the guardian of their treasures.

TUATHA DÉ DANANN: A powerful tribe who defeated the Fomorians in battle and became the gods of ancient Ireland. Some of the best-known members of the Tuatha Dé Danann include: The Dagda, The Morrigan (cool/scary goddess of war), Manannán Mac Lir and Brigid.

UAITHNE: One of the three treasures that belonged to The Dagda. *Uaithne* was the harp of power that could control the thoughts and feelings of anyone who heard its music. The other two treasures were *Coire Ansic,* a cauldron that never grew empty, and *Lorg Mór,* a spear that could kill nine people in a single blow. When The Dagda went to the Otherworld with the rest of the Tuatha Dé Danann, he left the treasures with Aoife for safekeeping, in case he should ever have need of them again.

Read an extract from Cat and Shane's

first adventure, *The Book of Secrets*

CHAPTER ONE

Once a Witch ...

Now that the rain had finally stopped, Cat and her friends were allowed outside for eleven o'clock break for the first time in what felt like forever. When the bell rang, the whole class jumped to their feet and charged for the door, ignoring Mr Brennan's shouted reminder to stick to the schoolyard because the field was still wet and boggy after the latest downpour.

Cat hoped the drier weather would last throughout the weekend because tomorrow was Halloween and she had plans. Top of the list was trick-or-treating. Now that she was eleven years old she was painfully aware that her trick-or-treating days were numbered so she made a solemn promise to herself to make the most of it this year ... just in case. After they had their fill of chocolate and sweets, she and her friends would pay a visit to the local bonfire. Some of the older children had been stockpiling wood for the past few weeks and the word around town was that it would be the biggest bonfire Clonbridge had ever seen. Of course, that was the rumour every year and every year it was much the same – a mildly disappointing affair broken up by the Gardaí as soon as the first crack of a firework was heard. It didn't matter, Cat was still excited. Halloween was her absolute favourite time of year.

The only downside to her plans was that she had to bring her baby brother Mikey along. Mikey was fifteen months old and couldn't walk for very long before crying that he wanted to be carried. Cat tried to protest that Mikey was too small to appreciate Halloween, but her mam had stood firm, saying that Mikey deserved to join in the fun and reminding her that she didn't have time to bring him herself.

'You know I have my classes on Saturdays, Kitty-Cat,' she said, ignoring Cat's scowl at the use of her hated nickname. 'Please, I really need to you to help me out. You only need to bring him up and down the street and then you'll have the rest of the evening with your friends, I promise. Besides, Granny will be around if you need anything.'

'If Granny's there to watch Mikey, then why do *I* have to bring him at all?'

Her mam didn't answer. She just gave Cat one of her legendary *because-I-said-so* stares that meant the conversation was over.

Cat's sense of injustice deepened when her mam returned from the shops the following day with two costumes – a plastic Batman outfit for Mikey and a pointed witch's hat for her.

'But I was a witch last year. I wanted to go as a haunted doll this time!' she said with indignation.

'I know, Cat, but I couldn't get to the shops any earlier and they were sold out of almost everything,' said her mam as she tried to feed a protesting Mikey, who, on top of being the most annoying baby in the world, was also fussy around food. 'You'll have to just make do.'

Before Cat could formulate a suitable reply, her mam had turned away to tend to Mikey who was sobbing over his upended bowl of Coco Pops.

Just like that it was settled. She would be bringing Mikey trick-or-treating and, once again, she would be dressed as a witch.

After a quick detour to the school's library room to return the book she had borrowed, *Halloween Through the Ages*, Cat stepped out into the yard and spotted her friends huddled in a circle by the fence.

'Cat!' Jess shrieked happily. 'Come join us. We're telling scary stories.'

'Karol was telling us about knick-knacks,' added Sarah, Jess's twin sister who had been born five minutes before her and clung to the title of 'older sister' fiercely, always cutting across her twin whenever possible.

'*Nocnica*,' corrected Karol, blushing slightly to find himself the centre of attention. Karol was a quiet Polish boy who had moved to Clonbridge last year. He was nice, but painfully shy. When the twins noticed he spent most of his time alone they quickly co-opted him into their friend group.

'Whatever,' said Jess, rolling her eyes with exaggeration. 'Go on then, tell us more about them.'

'Well,' he said slowly, 'my brother Lukasz says they come

to your room at night when you're asleep and sit on your chest and suck your soul out of your mouth. Lukasz says that's why you should always sleep on your side. They can't steal your soul when you're on your side.'

'That's stupid,' said Shane, a tall, freckled boy who was leaning against the fence reading a comic and eavesdropping on their conversation as always. She wondered why he even bothered. Cat knew for a fact he didn't like her, and she suspected he didn't like her friends much either. Shane didn't seem to like anything.

'I don't think anyone asked your opinion,' said Sarah, shooting Shane an angry look. 'Go on, Karol, how else can you stop the *Nocnica*?'

'Well,' said Karol, eyeing Shane warily, 'a stone with a hole in it can make them disappear. I don't know why …'

Shane snorted again, 'So what, you just carry a stone with a hole in it around with you all the time? That's so dumb.'

'Oh, shut *up*, Shane!' snapped Ebele. 'I want to hear what Karol's saying.'

Ebele was the daughter of the town's doctor. She was the smartest kid in class by far, as well as one of the kindest.

She rarely got mad, but when she did, everyone tended to listen. Shane opened his mouth as if to say something else, but finding four angry girls glaring back at him, he thought better of it and leaned back against the fence in a huff.

'Have you ever seen one?' Ebele asked, leaning forward in excitement.

'I think they're only in Poland,' said Karol with a shrug.

'I've seen a Banshee,' said Cat and almost immediately regretted it. She hadn't meant to tell anyone that.

They all turned to stare at her, even Shane.

'Did you really?' asked Jess. 'No messing?'

Cat nodded. 'Last year, on the night my granddad died. Me and Mam and Mikey had been staying over at Granny and Granddad's house at the time because he was really sick and the doctors said he probably wouldn't, you know …'

Cat trailed off. She didn't like thinking about that time when everyone was so sad and she hadn't known how to help.

'Anyway, it was the middle of the night and this weird screeching sound woke me up. It was coming from outside and it was the worst noise I've ever heard, like a fork scraping on a plate or …'

'Or Mrs Quinn's singing!' said Sarah, causing them all to erupt into gales of laughter. Mrs Quinn was the teacher in charge of the school choir and her enthusiasm for singing was as great as her voice was terrible.

Cat smiled and continued. 'When I heard the noise, I ran to the window and saw a woman outside the house. There was something strange about her, almost like she wasn't fully there. She was just sort of floating there above the ground. And her eyes …' Cat shuddered. What could she say about her eyes? They were totally empty and darker than the sky on a starless night. Looking into them was like staring into a bottomless pit. 'When she looked up at me, I thought I was going to die.'

'What happened next?' asked Ebele in an almost-whisper.

'I thought I was having a nightmare at first, but then the door banged open and Granny was standing there with a face like thunder. She ran to the window and yelled at the Banshee.'

'She didn't!' said Jess.

Cat nodded. 'She did. She said, "*You've already got him,*

you old crone, now away with you!" but that's my Granny for you.'

Cat's friends nodded sagely. They were all familiar with Granny Mary and could well imagine her threatening a supernatural being.

'Granny told me to go back to sleep and when I woke up the next morning, Granddad was gone.'

For a moment, no one said anything. Cat looked down at her feet. She hadn't meant to make things awkward. Suddenly, the bell rang out, breaking the silence and summoning them all back to class. Reluctantly, they trudged toward the building.

'Did you really see a Banshee?' asked Shane, slowing down to walk beside Cat.

'Maybe,' she said carefully, 'or maybe I'm just trying to freak you all out before Halloween.'

Shane rolled his eyes. 'I knew it,' he muttered and stalked off.

But it wasn't a lie. Cat really *had* seen a Banshee. Or at least, she thought she had. It had been so long since she had seen the pale woman, she was starting to doubt it had really happened at all. Granny never doubted though. A few days after Granddad's funeral she sat Cat down and told her she had 'the Sight', just like all the other women in the family.

Well, *almost* all the women. Cat's mam didn't believe in the Sight and would give out to Granny every time she brought it up, telling her to stop filling Cat's head with nonsense.

'Every so often the Sight skips a generation,' Granny said with a sniff. 'I blame your granddad, bless his soul. He was a lovely man, but he wanted for a bit of imagination.'

Ever since then it had been their secret and, truth be told, it was the reason Cat was so excited for Halloween this year – she could finally swap ghost and fairy stories with Granny without her mam pursing her lips in disapproval.

The rest of the afternoon passed in a pleasant haze. It was almost midterm break, so Mr Brennan decided to take it easy on the class. Instead of their usual Friday maths and spelling lessons, he allowed them to spend an hour painting Halloween-inspired pictures. Cat painted a creepy doll with haunted eyes and sighed. *Maybe next year …*